Meet the team:

Alex – A quiet lad from ▓▓▓▓▓▓▓▓▓▓, Alex leads the team in survival skills. His dad is in the SAS and Alex is determined to follow in his footsteps, whatever it takes. He who dares . . .

Li – Expert in martial arts and free-climbing, Li can get to grips with most situations . . .

Paulo – The laid-back Argentinian is a mechanical genius, and with his medical skills he can patch up injuries as well as motors . . .

Hex – An ace hacker, Hex is first rate at code-breaking and can bypass most security systems . . .

Amber – Her top navigational skills mean the team are rarely lost. Rarely lost for words either, rich-girl Amber can show some serious attitude . . .

With plenty of hard work and training, together they are Alpha Force – an elite squad of young people dedicated to combating injustice throughout the world.

In *Blood Money* Alpha Force are in southern India racing against time to save a young kidnap victim . . .

www.**kidsatrandomhouse**.co.uk/alphaforce

CHRIS RYAN

ALPHA FORCE

RYAN

BLOOD MONEY

RED
FOX

ALPHA FORCE: BLOOD MONEY
978 0 0994 8014 3 from January 2007
A RED FOX BOOK 0 099 48014 X
First published in Great Britain by Red Fox,
an imprint of Random House Children's Books

This edition published 2005

3 5 7 9 10 8 6 4

Papers used by Random House Children's Books are natural, recyclable
products made from wood grown in sustainable forests. The manufacturing
processes conform to the environmental regulations of the country of origin.

Typeset in Sabon by Palimpsest Book Production Limited,
Polmont, Stirlingshire

Red Fox Books are published by Random House Children's Books,
61–63 Uxbridge Road, London W5 5SA,
a division of The Random House Group Ltd,
in Australia by Random House Australia (Pty) Ltd,
20 Alfred Street, Milsons Point, Sydney, NSW 2061, Australia,
in New Zealand by Random House New Zealand Ltd,
18 Poland Road, Glenfield, Auckland 10, New Zealand,
and in South Africa by Random House (Pty) Ltd,
Isle of Houghton, Corner Boundary Road & Carse O'Gowrie,
Houghton 2198, South Africa.

THE RANDOM HOUSE GROUP Limited Reg. No. 954009
www.kidsatrandomhouse.co.uk

A CIP catalogue record for this book is available from the British Library.

Printed and bound in Great Britain by
Cox & Wyman Ltd, Reading, Berkshire

ALPHA FORCE

The field of operation...

PROLOGUE: THE KIDNEY MAN

Tagore Trilok followed the manservant down the dark corridor. The servant's leather sandals squeaked faintly, but otherwise his feet made no sound on the plush red carpet. They were in a mansion on the outskirts of Chennai, southern India, the home of a rich man. The walls were dark mahogany panels. A golden cobra stood on a chest, looming out of the rich-coloured wood, its hood spread like a threat. The ceiling fan above beat a moving shadow on the cobra like swaying palm fronds. Trilok reckoned the snake must be solid gold.

Above the sound of the servant's sandals, another noise was growing louder. Once Trilok had noticed it, he couldn't hear anything else but the wet, liquid gurgle. He shuddered.

It was the sound of a man's blood being pumped out of his body and around a machine.

The servant opened the doors at the end of the corridor – big double doors. The bedroom was large, another rich haven of mahogany, with yellow silk at the windows. There was a solid bed, decorated with intricate carvings and littered with brocaded cushions. In the bed was a small figure, as dark and still as the mahogany around him.

This was the client.

He seemed to be sleeping, but Trilok's eyes were drawn to the dialysis machine – a white unit just over a metre high, with a screen and knobs and dials. It was such a bleak piece of laboratory equipment, out of place in the finely furnished room. Tubes ran from it and under the silk bedcovers. Trilok knew they went into a hole in the man's abdomen. The tubes were dark – dark with the blood that was flowing out of the man's veins. It passed through all the filters and machinery inside that white metal tower and eventually returned to his body. His kidneys had failed, and every drop of blood had to flow through that metal vampire. It sucked out the impurities that his body could no longer remove.

The machine hummed and churned like a fridge. No matter how often he saw it, the process put a chill in Trilok's heart. And he saw it often. All his clients depended on these cold machines. They wanted him to find them a kidney so that they could have a transplant and live a normal life again.

The man in the bed stirred and opened his eyes.

The servant spoke. 'Sahib, Mr Trilok to see you.'

The man sat up carefully, so as not to dislodge the tubes. 'About time, Mr Trilok. You were supposed to come this morning.' Although he looked weak his voice had an edge of anger. He dismissed the servant with a wave of his hand.

When they were alone, Trilok said, 'I'm sorry I couldn't keep our earlier appointment, Mr Gopal. How are you?'

The man snapped back at him, 'How do you think? Look at me.'

Trilok swallowed. Sometimes the clients were abrupt. Particularly the high-caste ones. Trilok smiled apologetically; tried to look gracious. 'Hopefully I can help you, Mr Gopal.'

Gopal shifted position in the bed, his eyes rolling as though he had already tired of the meeting. 'I don't want empty promises, Trilok. This won't be easy. I've already had a kidney transplant but it was unsuccessful. I want another but the doctors say it could take years to find a match because the first transplant ruined my immune system.' He moved again, his eyes screwed up with pain. When they opened again, Trilok noticed that the brown irises were surrounded by yellowed whites. His clients always looked like this. The pollutants built up in their bodies and seeped into their eyes like a stain.

Trilok answered patiently, 'I will do my best, sahib. But it's more difficult. Your immune system is more sensitive since the first transplant was rejected. Now not as many people will match you.'

Gopal waved his hand, like he did when he was

dismissing the servant. 'That's why I'm paying you to find one. And do it quickly. I can't wait for years. I'm an important man. I can't live like this. Look at me. I'm tied to this machine. I have to keep still for hours. I'm in pain.'

Trilok started thinking aloud. 'I can start by calling some moneylenders; they go around the villages and they know who can't pay their debts. Usually somebody is willing to sell—'

Gopal cut him off. 'I don't care what you have to do. Just get me a kidney. I don't care where you get it, so long as it's a live donor. A nice, healthy live donor. No dead bodies, do you hear? Don't try to cheat me – I know transplants from dead bodies don't take so well.'

Trilok nodded. 'Absolutely, sahib. I only deal in live donors.'

Gopal lay back and stared at the ceiling, his small head and shoulders almost engulfed by the embroidered cushions. 'I have rung for my man. He will see you out. Wait there until he comes. I don't want you wandering about the house.' He closed his eyes.

The only sound in the room was the gentle beat

of the ceiling fan and the wet pulse of the machine as it sucked Gopal's blood out of him and pumped it back in.

Trilok looked out of the window. Outside, the vast lawn was bathed in brilliant sunshine. Two sprinkler hoses snaked across the emerald grass, throwing long bright arcs of water from side to side like whips.

1

SNAKE

The snake slithered out of the upturned pot. Its head was a pale brown arrow covered in prehistoric scales. The coils of its body followed swiftly, slithering out like a falling rope. A cobra, released from captivity into a crowd of parents and children and teenaged aid volunteers enjoying a simple festival at the village shrine.

A cobra. The five volunteers froze in horror. Alex, Li, Paulo, Hex and Amber – Alpha Force – were highly trained in the arts of survival; they knew how deadly the cobra was. Would the noisy crowd scare the snake away? Or would it strike? There were bare legs just metres away from its questing tongue. Children squatted on the ground, drawing pictures in the earth with their fingers and laughing. They were easy targets. Who would the snake go for?

Normally Alpha Force would have taken charge: told everyone to keep absolutely still, or cleared the area. But the snake had been released deliberately. A man in straw-coloured shorts and a crumpled shirt had stepped forward with an earthenware water pot. The crowd had cleared around him and he'd lowered it gently to the ground, put it on its side and removed the plug so that the snake could slide out onto the sun-baked ground. And when the snake came out the spectators smiled and welcomed it.

Right now, all over India, Hindus were celebrating the cobra, symbol of fertility and manifestation of Lord Shiva. However hair-raising it might look, Alpha Force had to trust that they knew what they were doing.

Li was calmer than the others. Her parents were naturalists and had worked with a wide variety of dangerous animals. She guessed that a cobra confronted by a crowd would sidle off into the undergrowth. And then the festivities could continue safely.

But the snake made no attempt to escape. Its tongue flicked in and out, a slender black fork tasting the air; its flinty eyes took in the colourful skirts, the dusty feet, the jangling jewellery, the laughing faces. Then suddenly it reared up, spreading its hood wide like a fan.

Now this looked a lot more dangerous.

Li dug her slender fingers into Paulo's arm. The snake's head was raised a good forty centimetres in the air, its body curled in a wide muscular arc on the ground. The back of its hood was dark brown, with black and white markings like a set of ferocious eyes.

Beside Li, Paulo was just as tense. He knew exactly what she was thinking, because he was thinking the same. He'd grown up among animals too, on a ranch in Argentina. He knew that frightened animals had two ways of coping: run away or attack. That snake had no intention of moving away.

So there was only one thing for it to do: lash out. Should he do something? Had the simple festival just gone badly wrong?

The children squatted on their haunches, looking at the snake, their big brown eyes full of wonder. Three women dropped to their knees in front of it. They brought their hands forward as though praying – just centimetres away from the rearing body. They didn't even look at the deadly predator, but bowed their heads.

Their colourful shawls, one green, one blue, one pink, made easy targets. Paulo and Li instinctively drew closer together and held their breath. This was madness; it contradicted everything they knew about survival. Should they stop it now?

The women began to rock backwards and forwards, chanting. The crowd joined in and soon everyone was softly singing a rhythmic, gentle Hindu song.

The snake was poised above the women, only inches away from their heads. It swayed gently, its tongue flashing in and out. Its black eyes, like tiny points of obsidian, gazed inscrutably at them. The mirrors sewn into the women's colourful robes threw flashes of light onto it as they moved and their silver bangles jingled. All of these things might provoke it to attack. But the snake did not strike.

Alex, next to Paulo and Li, was just as horrified. He knew that the striking range of the cobra was the raised part of its body. So anyone within forty centimetres could be dead. Survival lore had been as much a part of his upbringing as maths and football. His dad was in the SAS and from an early age Alex had been fascinated by the outdoors, camping out regularly in his native Northumbria. He always had a knife at his belt and a survival kit in his pocket. He could hear his father's voice as though he were beside him right now: *If you disturb a snake, stay very still until it's gone away.* If he was here he'd be having kittens. The praying women were at most thirty centimetres away from the cobra's taut body. Their unprotected arms were almost touching it. Alex looked at all the bare feet, bare arms, bare legs. If he was going anywhere near hostile wildlife he wore long trousers and sturdy boots. His instincts were screaming, *No, no, no.*

Hex, next to Alex, was gripping Amber's shoulder so hard he thought he must be bruising it badly. But he couldn't help it. If he ever got that close to a cobra he would not be kneeling in front of it humming to himself.

None of the team dared move in case they broke the spell and it all went wrong. Now some of the children were tossing crimson flower petals at the snake, their mouths open in delight. The snake's tongue continued to flick. Others threw uncooked rice. Amber flinched as the hard grains hit the snake's taut body. Surely that would provoke it to strike?

A faint breeze wafted a stream of dust over the dry, sandy earth. It collected on Alex's pale, sweat-soaked face like a velvety dusting. It frosted Amber's ebony skin like talcum powder; settled like fine ash in Li's inky-black plait of hair; formed a light covering on Paulo's springy curls; made Hex squeeze his green eyes into a squint. The snake spread its hood even further, the markings opening out like widened eyes. Its body followed the movements of the chanting crowd.

Slowly, as the chanting and the worshipping went on, and the snake stood accepting it, Alpha Force began to realize that the snake presented no threat; they relaxed and started to enjoy the spectacle.

Paulo, used to handling big, unpredictable animals on his parents' ranch, was the first to go with the flow. Animals could always surprise you. You always had to be on your guard, but there was something mesmeric about the tall, dignified snake, the markings moving like a slow, hypnotic dream. A grin spread across Paulo's handsome features. This was awesome.

Li was more logical. This shouldn't be happening. Perhaps the snake's instincts to flee and to kill were cancelling each other out, so that it couldn't move. Its stillness made her think of the state of calm she felt when doing martial arts. She could be calm, balanced and focused while delivering devastating kicks and turning like a whiplash. When she was doing gymnastics or climbing – her other great passions – she always remained cool, however demanding the move, however vast the drop beneath her. When Li concentrated like that, it was as if time stood still. To see it in the snake was wonderful. But that didn't mean it wasn't the freakiest thing ever.

Hex was just as impressed, but he definitely liked to keep dangerous creatures safely on the other side of a computer screen. Not that he spent much time playing games; particularly not since Alpha Force had brought him more real-life adventure than he ever thought he'd see. Hex's real element was cyber-space, at the keyboard of his state-of-the-art palmtop. When Hex surfed, he had a magic touch. He could go wherever he wanted. There wasn't a code he couldn't break, a firewall he couldn't breach, a file he couldn't tease open.

Amber thought that if someone had described to her what she was seeing now, she simply wouldn't have believed them. All the villagers were so calm, as though it never occurred to them that the snake could harm them. And the cobra was serenely accepting its due. Amber was an experienced horse rider, and understood how deeply the handler's attitude affected the animal. Could it simply be this belief that was winning through? It was a humbling lesson.

Humbling; Amber smiled to herself as she thought it. Brought up by billionaire parents in the USA and used to the high life, she realized that humble wasn't a word her friends would have thought was even in her vocabulary. But life had changed Amber over the past few years: her parents had died, and then she had discovered that they were working undercover to help disadvantaged people. She had been marooned on a desert island with the four friends who stood beside her now. What they went through there – their battle to survive – had forged a bond as unbreakable as Hex's claw-like grip on her shoulder. Each of them, Amber, Li, Paulo, Hex and Alex, discovered they had remarkable potential. They came away fired with a desire to make a difference in the world, and to carry on the work started by Amber's parents. Alpha Force would look for injustice and try to help people.

They were in Nayla, in southern India, on an aid project, helping to build a school. It had all started when Alex, at home in Northumberland and grappling with maths homework, saw a TV programme about poverty in the tiny villages all over India. Aid projects had brought clean water, electricity and communal telephones; but the villagers couldn't make further progress into the twenty-first century because they had no schools. A reporter had gone to a village and learned that if the children wanted to go to school they had to walk eight kilometres and miss a day's work in the paddy fields – which the community couldn't afford. Alex had scribbled down the web link to the aid organization and e-mailed the others: *You remember that money we raised last summer in the adventure race? How about if we helped to build a school in India?*

After months of preparation, they were here in Nayla. The village was exactly as he had seen it on the TV: the clutch of houses made of earth and stone, with whitewashed walls and grey tiled roofs, surrounded by fertile rice fields; the standpipe providing the water supply; the sun that beat down despite the dramatic clouds; the shrine where they were now all gathered – a termite mound surrounded by a low wall of red-painted bricks and crowned with marigolds. Except the emerald paddy fields were now parched like straw, waiting for the rains.

And now a small building site stood a hundred metres from the shrine. Four pallets of plastic-wrapped breeze blocks surrounded a concrete slab they had laid that morning to become the foundations. A small wooden hut like a garden shed formed a tool store. Scaffolding poles lay ready to be assembled.

Alex felt pleased as he looked at it: their efforts in the adventure race had bought building materials and plans and paid for a foreman. Alpha Force would provide most of the labour and the villagers would join in when they could. Originally they'd had two other workers, including a builder, from an aid organization, but they had both come down with severe food poisoning a week ago and an ambulance had taken them back to Chennai. The project was now behind schedule. Fortunately the hard work of planning and laying the foundations was done. Now Alpha Force just had to get the walls up and the roof on before the rains hit.

Hex had said that the monsoon would start within days. He'd checked it on the government weather database. Not the ordinary website that everybody consulted – that one was a few days out of date. The site Hex had found was the secret one that used military satellites. The monsoon was visible as a vast black shadow advancing across the subcontinent. They didn't have long. And that was if they survived the snake ceremony . . .

2
BUSINESS AS USUAL

The ceremony was finishing. The man in straw-coloured shorts and tunic squatted on the ground, grasped the cobra by the tail and lifted it. The cobra writhed as it found itself in mid-air, its graceful head swaying as though held on a wire. In the blink of an eye the man lowered the snake inside the earthenware pot and put the lid on.

Li watched with alarm. 'What will they do with that snake?'

A girl answered, 'My father will set it free in the fields.'

Alex recognized the girl, and her father beside her. He had seen them on the documentary. Naresh, the father, had been pictured on a tractor, clearing irrigation ditches; Bina, twelve years old, was filmed in a turquoise sari stepping like an exotic bird through the deep green paddy fields, tending the plants. She talked about how she longed to learn to use computers. She was wearing that same turquoise sari today. It was strange to recognize them from a TV programme aired months ago and half a world away.

'How do you avoid being bitten?' said Li.

'When the god is there we can worship without fear,' said Bina. 'That is the ceremony.'

'But now,' smiled Naresh, 'we are very, very careful.'

Around them, the women who had been bowing before the snake were now on their feet, dusting down their clothes. Alex quietly pointed out to the others someone else he recognized from the programme: Bina's mother, Mootama, in a green sari.

Like a flock of birds on the move, the women hitched up their skirts and turned towards the fields, their bangles jangling like wind chimes. Time to go back to work.

'Come on, guys,' said Alex. 'Let's see how much of the walls we can get done before Pradesh gets back.' Pradesh was the foreman. Normally he would be there but he had bad toothache and was seeing the dentist in Chennai.

'I'll mix the mortar,' said Li, and hurried over to the hut to fetch tools and materials.

'I'll get water for you,' said Amber. She grabbed a bucket and went to a water container they had filled earlier in the day.

'Paulo,' said Alex, 'you find the plans and work out where the first wall goes; Hex and I can be a human chain passing you breeze blocks.'

Hex tried to tear the plastic wrapping off the concrete blocks, but it was too tough. Alex saw him in difficulties and passed him the knife he wore at his belt. The five worked seamlessly as a team. Their experience of building camps in terrain as varied as the rainforest and the desert, and of generally looking after each other on missions, meant they could anticipate each other's needs perfectly.

Paulo, the plans in one hand and a water bottle in the other, was pacing out the distance from the front wall to the corridor partition. A small black dog was following him. Its bones were clearly visible through its skin – it looked in terrible condition, but it seemed docile enough. Li, measuring out mortar, watched, amused. Animals always loved Paulo. Here was a wild dog, trotting up to him as meekly as though he had trained it from birth. Paulo could probably charm cobras out of the fields and persuade them to climb into pots all by themselves, she thought, although she would never have said anything of the sort to his face.

Hex's mind was on the snake. To his logical brain, Bina's explanation did not compute. 'What do you reckon, Alex? How did they make that snake stay there? Was it hypnotized by the chanting?'

It was Amber, carrying a water bucket, who answered. 'Snakes don't have ears, dumb-ass.' She tweaked his ear with her free hand.

'I wasn't asking you,' said Hex, and poked her with a stick.

'Well, it must be like what snake charmers do,'

said Amber. She twirled her fingers in front of Hex's face like a stage magician. '*Trust in me*,' she began to sing softly.

Hex pulled a face. 'If I was your snake and I saw you doing that, I'd stay in my basket and never come out.'

'You wouldn't like to be my snake?' teased Amber.

Hex hissed back at her. 'Could you handle my venom?'

Li joined in. 'I think she'd take out your fangs and starve you,' she said. 'That's what real snake charmers do.'

Amber gave a yowl of laughter. 'Good idea!' She took the water to Li and mixed it into the dry mortar while Li sealed the remaining mortar in its bag.

The black dog was trotting along at Paulo's heels as he paced. 'Do you want some water?' he grinned. He poured a little puddle from his water bottle onto the concrete.

The dog went rigid, as though its whole body was electrified. Saliva poured from its mouth.

Li had spotted it. 'Paulo, get away,' she shrieked. 'It's got rabies!'

The dog sprang towards Paulo, its dripping jaws open. Rabies. The word rang in his mind like a shrill alarm. If the dog bit him – and if he couldn't get to a hospital quickly enough – he would die a horrible, painful death. The jaws snapped at him. He thrust the plastic water bottle in their way. The teeth clamped down hard and crushed it. Paulo ran.

Although his tactic had saved him from a bite, the water made the dog's throat and chest go into agonizing spasms. It let out a vicious snarl, fixed its eyes on Paulo and streaked after him.

There was no chance that Paulo could outrun the dog: four legs always win against two. Li scooped up the heavy wooden board holding the mortar and hurled it at the dog, knocking the animal over. It soon scrambled upright, paws slipping in the mortar, but Paulo had time to duck round the pallet of breeze blocks where Hex and Alex were standing. Which meant it would go for one of the others.

Li vaulted up onto the other pallet and crouched like a cat waiting to pounce. Amber was the nearest to the dog now. Its dark eyes fixed on her as it scrabbled off the wet mortar. As Amber raced towards the breeze blocks, Li put her hand down to help her up. She was much smaller than the black American girl. Could she stay upright as Amber took hold? The dog was now a mere stride behind. If Amber failed to jump up first time, the dog would get her. Amber put her hand in Li's and sprang for the top of the pile of blocks, and like a pair of circus performers they did it in one smooth move. The dog cannoned into the pile and Li backed away from the edge, pulling Amber with her.

On the other side of the site, Alex, Hex and Paulo crouched behind another pallet. For the moment it seemed the girls were safe. Paulo called out to them: 'Don't get any of that saliva on you. It's full of viruses.'

'Brilliant,' Amber hissed under her breath. 'Thanks a lot.'

The dog stood on its back legs, baying for its quarry and spraying saliva every time it moved its head.

Amber looked at Li. 'It can't climb, can it?'

Before she could answer, the dog sprang up, front claws outstretched. The two girls huddled tightly, making themselves as small as possible. The dog's claws met slippery plastic and it slid down again.

'I was going to say it can't,' gasped Li. 'But it's angry. It might do anything.'

Amber dug her nail into the plastic wrapping by her feet. It seemed pretty strong. 'Thank heavens for packaging that ruins your fingernails. I always knew there was some point to it.'

The dog sprang up again. There was a ripping sound as the plastic gave way.

'Next time it will be up here,' said Li. 'Quick.'

They dropped off the other side. The dog scrambled up on top of the blocks just as the girls hit the ground and ran.

Meanwhile Alex looked for a weapon. What did they have? A big pile of breeze blocks. They were too heavy to throw over any distance. There were some long metal scaffolding poles piled near the foundation slab. To his left was the tool shed. 'We'll herd it into there,' he said to the others.

Paulo touched Hex's arm. 'Let's get some scaffolding poles.' The two boys sprinted towards the pile of metal poles.

Li and Amber heard the dog land. It must have taken an enormous leap from the breeze blocks, because it was now barely centimetres behind them. Their lungs were bursting as they dragged in hot, dusty air, pumping their legs hard and fast to stay ahead.

Alex pulled open the door to the hut. Li and Amber understood. They headed for it, the dog at their heels. At the last minute they dodged behind the door. The dog stopped, confused.

Then it focused on Alex, standing beside the door. It started towards him.

Alex retreated behind the door. The dog drew back; its quarry had vanished. But Alex didn't let that lull him into a sense of false security. It was still dangerous. He moved the door to keep its attention.

Behind the dog, Hex and Paulo moved stealthily in, their scaffold poles pointing at the dog like spears.

The dog sensed the movement behind. It whirled round and saw Hex and Paulo. It was surrounded.

'Now!' called Alex. 'Get it in the shed.'

Hex and Paulo lunged towards the dog. Paulo's

feet met the bag of mortar lying on the ground were Li had tied it. Normally he would have stayed upright but the pole unbalanced him. He crashed to the ground.

The dog spotted the circle's weakest member. It leaped in for the kill.

Paulo landed on his back. Instinct made him protect his inner organs and he squirmed around like a swimmer doing a tumble turn. The dog's feet missed him as he rolled, but he smelled fetid breath, glimpsed yellowed teeth and a red, curling tongue swimming in saliva.

Paulo seized the bag of mortar and held it to his chest like a solid pillow. The dog landed on him, squashing all the air from his lungs. He heard muffled sounds as it sank its teeth into the mortar bag. Had he been unprotected, the bite would have ripped out his throat. But he was still trapped, pinned by the weight of the dog and the heavy bag. He jerked to try to dislodge the dog, but the jaws were digging into the bag. All Paulo could do was shield as much of himself as possible. The dog dug furiously, ripping through the bag, the deadly saliva soaking into the mortar. Very soon, it would bite through.

Then Paulo felt a harder blow. And another. This is it, he thought. Another.

The dog stopped its terrible snarling and lay still.

Someone pushed the dog and the bag off him and dragged him to his feet. Alex. He had a spade in his hand which he'd used to lever the dog off without touching it.

'Are you all right?'

Paulo was breathing hard. 'Think so. What happened?'

Hex was picking up two halves of a broken concrete block. 'The dog got in the way of a breeze block.'

Paulo looked at the dog. It lay awkwardly, its head gashed, blood welling up through the patchy black fur. The saliva continued to pour from its jaws like water bubbling from a spring. It mixed with the mortar from the split bag to make a grey mud. 'Is it dead?'

'I wouldn't guarantee it,' said Li. 'Probably stunned. Come on, let's get away.'

Paulo looked around in confusion. 'Aren't we going to do something with it? Should we put it in the shed?'

'No,' said Li sharply. She pulled him away. 'We mustn't touch it.'

Then Paulo noticed the crowd that had gathered. But unlike before, this was just the men of the village. They advanced on the little party. 'Are you all right?' called Naresh. 'Did it bite you?'

Paulo looked at his hands, his arms, his feet as if to check. He shook his head. 'No, no, it didn't.' He glanced at the dog. It was starting to twitch, as though coming to.

Amber saw that Naresh had a rock in his hand. She looked at the other earnest faces around him. They also held rocks and their eyes were narrowed with purpose.

'Come on,' she said to the others. 'I think they've got this under control.'

They walked away down the road. As they went, the crowd closed on the dog and pelted it with stones.

Amber winced and looked away. She was upset.

'It's the best thing for it,' said Li. 'A quick death rather than a slow, agonized one. Rabies is a horrific way to die.'

Alex put his arm around Amber. 'And Hex stunned it so it won't feel anything.'

'But I can't understand it,' said Paulo. 'I thought dogs with rabies were always aggressive. This one looked as gentle as a lamb.'

'Rabies can look like that,' said Li. 'You should be careful of any wild animal that's more docile than you'd expect. It's because the virus makes them run down and ill.' She raised her eyes and cursed herself. 'Damn,' she said quietly. 'I should have remembered.' But there was no time for recriminations; something more urgent had to be done. 'Guys, I don't want to alarm you but we'd better check ourselves very carefully for injuries. And nobody touch your eyes, nose or mouth, just in case you've got some of that dog's saliva on your hands.'

'Oh that's brilliant,' said Amber. 'There was so much of it flying about we've probably got it everywhere.'

3
BRIDE BURNING

Back in their quarters, a simple house rented by the aid project, Paulo peeled off his clothes, making sure he didn't touch the outside. His white shirt and pale shorts bore mud-coloured smears. It was all over his arms and legs. Was it infected mortar or just plain old-fashioned mud?

In the girls' room, Li and Amber got undressed too. Amber looked down at her navy blue long-sleeved shirt and Capri pants. 'You'd better not tell me we have to burn these. That's half my wardrobe for this trip.'

'We should be OK if we dunk them in antiseptic and wash them,' said Li. She picked up her clothes with a stick and tossed them outside, then did Amber's. They wrapped themselves in towels and went out to the bathing area, a red canvas cubicle behind the building with an improvised shower made from a hose and a hand pump. There was another area for the boys.

Alex and Hex were outside on the veranda, which ran the length of the house. Alex had mixed up an antiseptic solution in a big brass bowl with boiled water and some crystals of potassium permanganate from his survival kit. The liquid glowed rose in the golden interior of the bowl.

With a pair of sticks, Hex picked up each garment in turn and dropped it into the solution, poking it well under the water. After it had soaked he scrubbed it with a stiff brush to remove the grit and mud, then hooked it out and passed it to Alex, who rinsed it and hung it over the veranda balustrade. Soon a line of shirts, shorts and trousers were hung out.

As Hex scrubbed at a pair of shorts, he saw that

the group of men who had come to help them were making their way back to the fields. A plume of smoke rose into the air. He handed Alex the shorts. 'Looks like they're burning the dog.'

'Very sensible,' said Alex, and took the shorts to rinse.

Hex got to work on a shirt and heard Alex say, 'Oh dear.'

He looked up. 'What?'

Alex was holding out the shorts. 'Do you think these have changed colour?'

Hex looked at the shorts. They were a bit purply — not really vivid, but as though they had been soaked in berry juice. He didn't remember anyone wearing shorts that colour today. 'What colour were they before?'

Alex thought. 'I think they were a bit less purple.'

'Oh just hang them up,' said Hex. 'The girls have got so many clothes I'm sure they won't mind if some of them turn a different colour.' He went back to scrubbing the shirt.

A howl of anguish made him jump out of his skin.

Paulo was standing behind him, wrapped in a towel. He was peering into the bowl where Hex was scrubbing, his wet hair curling into tight, mad corkscrews. 'My shirt!' he yelled.

Hex followed Paulo's gaze. The shirt in the bowl was looking a bit more rosy than he remembered. 'Oops,' said Hex and hooked it out.

Li heard Paulo's roar just as she got out of the shower. She wrapped herself in a towel and rushed to the veranda. Paulo was holding up his dripping shirt by its shoulders.

'*Madre di Dios!*' he exclaimed. 'It's pink!'

Certainly the shirt was a definite shade of rose.

Alex put a hand over his mouth. He really wanted to laugh but one look at Paulo's thunderous face made him think again.

Li reached out and fingered the shirt. 'Lovely colour.' Her hair was turbaned in another towel. It shook as she started to giggle.

'It's pink,' said Paulo again, loading the word with unmistakable loathing.

'Um, yes,' said Hex, 'I'm afraid it is. Sorry. But I had to get off all the icky stuff. It might wash out.'

Amber came out, fully dressed and tying a bandanna around her head. She had heard Hex's explanation through the window. 'I don't think that stuff will wash out. I splashed some on a white T-shirt and it wouldn't come out. But eventually it went brown.'

'There you are, Paulo,' said Hex. 'It'll go brown after a while. It probably oxidizes.'

Paulo looked sharply at Amber. 'How long will it take to go brown?'

Amber shrugged. 'I think it took a few weeks. Actually, I preferred the pink.'

'*Dios!*' snarled Paulo. He sounded rather like the rabid dog. He took the shirt and spread it out on the rail, refusing to look at any of the others.

'He's not happy,' said Li quietly. 'Not happy at all.'

'That,' whispered Alex to Li, 'is a very pink shirt.'

Back at the building site, Alpha Force buckled down to the task in hand. Soon the route of the walls was marked out with pegs, string and whitewash and it was time to lay the breeze blocks.

Amber, Hex and Alex started building the north end of the school; Li and Paulo took the south end. Then help arrived – four children who'd finished work in the fields came to see if they could lend a hand. Paulo split them into two teams, two girls against two boys, and told them to keep the supplies coming. Soon there was a friendly competition to see who could deliver bricks and mortar faster. The walls grew at a satisfying rate.

'There's something addictive about this,' said Li. She spread a line of mortar.

Paulo laid a block on it and squashed it down, squeezing out the surplus. 'I wouldn't expect a girl to like bricklaying.'

A dollop of mortar whizzed off Li's trowel and landed in a fat splat on his cheek. 'Macho pig.'

Paulo scraped the mortar off with his finger and leaned over to wipe it on her nose. Li dodged and hefted up the board with the mortar. She aimed it at his face, as though it was a custard pie. 'Don't escalate hostilities. You'll come off worse.' There wasn't much left on the board but it would make a satisfying mess.

'You want this?' It was the younger of the two Indian girls. She had brought another palette. A mass of freshly mixed mortar glistened like a cow pat on top.

Li eagerly swapped palettes with the girl. 'Thanks, Radha. Just what I need.' Radha was Bina's ten-year-old sister. Bina herself was over by the blocks, loading supplies into a wheelbarrow.

Li scooped up a big serving of mortar with her trowel. Paulo looked at her, challenging her to toss it at him. For a moment she looked as though she would, but at the last minute she flipped the trowel over and spread it for the next block.

Radha was watching, a frown on her face. 'Are you and Paulo married?'

'No way!' retorted Li scornfully.

Radha wasn't put off. 'I don't want to get married.'

Li spread another lick of mortar and Paulo put a brick on top. 'Why don't you want to get married?' As she said it she felt ancient. She must have heard the same old patronizing words from countless grandparents, aunts, uncles or friends of the family. Did I just say that? she thought.

'Because you need a dowry to get married,' said Radha. 'My parents will have to borrow money. If they don't give a big enough dowry and I am unlucky my new parents will set fire to me.'

Li still wasn't taking Radha totally seriously. 'Set fire to you?'

'There will be a fire in the kitchen and they won't be in time to save me.'

Paulo adjusted the fit of another block. 'I'm sure it won't be as bad as that.' *Dios*, now *he* felt like an ancient parent as well.

Bina had arrived with some more blocks. She set down the wheelbarrow. 'It might be that bad,' she said, and began to unload. Her face was deadly serious. 'It's called bride burning. It has happened to other girls around here. My mum said that's what happened to my aunt; she got married and they burned her. Then the man was free to marry again and get another dowry.'

Radha helped Bina take the blocks out of the wheelbarrow. 'Bina's got to get married soon,' she said.

'Yeah,' said Bina vehemently. 'I don't know what's going to happen. But I don't want to be burned.'

Li spread more mortar in silence. She was now quite ashamed that she had dismissed Radha's comments so lightly.

Paulo was quiet too. The girls were ten and twelve years old. He had sisters that age. All his sisters had to worry about was homework, exams, boys and music. Not marriage and finding a way to stop your new family killing you.

But as if that wasn't shocking enough, Radha's next words knocked them for six.

'Mum's going to sell a kidney.'

Bina snapped at her immediately, 'Radha, they don't want to know about that.' She unloaded the last block and picked up the handles of the barrow to move it.

'Yes we do,' said Li. The horror of the idea made the words come out sharply. 'What do you mean, she's going to sell a kidney?'

Bina sighed and glared at Radha as if cursing her. 'It's to pay our dowries.'

'How do you sell a kidney?' said Li.

Bina sighed, still holding the wheelbarrow handles. 'There's a man who comes; a moneylender.

He knows a man who gets kidneys for sick people. They buy kidneys from people like us.'

Paulo was horrified. 'But I don't understand. How will they buy your mother's kidney?'

Radha answered. 'She will go to a clinic in Chennai. She will have tests and then they will take out one of her kidneys.' It sounded so simple.

Li said, 'Can you live with just one kidney?'

Bina answered in a tight, tiny voice. 'I don't know.' She moved the wheelbarrow around swiftly and went to fetch more blocks.

4
A KIDNEY FOR SALE

Alex was still working with Amber and Hex at the north end of the site when a fat drop of water hit him on the forehead. He looked at the floor and saw another splodge, a large dark patch.

Hex looked up in disbelief, as though the dark clouds were directly contravening some law of physics. 'This shouldn't be happening. The satellite said the monsoon wasn't supposed to be here for seventy-two hours.'

'Well, that ceremony must have been a rain dance,

then,' rejoined Amber. A fat splodge of rain hit the back of her hand.

'Quick!' yelled Paulo from the other side of the site. 'Cover the walls!'

As one, they downed tools and raced for the shed. Alex hauled out a blue tarpaulin; Amber caught the tail end and the two young boys joined in, helping to carry it to one of the walls. Paulo and Li took the next tarpaulin and Hex brought up the rear with another, helped by Bina and Radha.

The heavens opened. It wasn't like rain, it was like a water tank bursting over their heads. It turned the sandy ground into slippery mud. Their clothes were soaked in seconds.

Alex tried heaving the tarpaulin up onto a wall, but the rain held it down and lashed his face like a thousand nails. It was like trying to climb a waterfall. Amber bashed the underside of the tarpaulin to tip out the water that had collected, but it just filled up again. The rain was so heavy she could scarcely see and the tarpaulin kept slipping, but she persevered. They had to cover the walls or the wet mortar would be washed away. They had made such good progress; the walls were now at shoulder height. It couldn't all be for nothing.

Finally, everyone regrouped in the middle of the foundation slab, their heads bowed to shield their eyes against the water. The walls were covered, the materials were protected. Nothing more could be done. The rain was so fierce it was roaring like thunder. Speaking was impossible. Paulo nodded towards the houses: *We go in and wait.*

The two young boys scampered away, delighted by the rain. People stood in the fields and outside their houses, their arms spread wide and their faces turned upwards. Bina and Radha hoisted up their saris to walk away, moving with difficulty as the wet fabric clung to their legs like bandages. As Paulo walked past them, Bina nodded to him. She had edged her eyes with kohl and the rain had spread it down her cheeks in tears of soot. The burning bride.

As soon as they got into their quarters, Hex went round the entire room peering at the ceiling. The others were peeling off sodden boots and socks, but not him.

Li wrung out her hair like a long black rope. 'Yuck,' she groaned. 'I am so wet.'

Alex looked out of the window. The view had vanished in a blur of rain. 'This is terrible. We were supposed to get the roof on before the monsoon.'

'This isn't the monsoon,' said Hex. He knelt to inspect a dark patch on the floor. 'It can't be.'

'Sure looks like a monsoon to me,' said Amber. 'What on earth are you doing?'

'Checking for leaks.' He straightened up. The patch on the floor wasn't wet. He had been so careful to pack his palmtop in waterproof plastic inside its carrying case, along with a sock to absorb any moisture. No way would he get it out if the roof was dripping. One more look upwards and he decided it would be OK. He got the palmtop out and powered up.

His fingers fluttered over the keyboard, looking for the weather satellites. The screen cast a green glow on his face, highlighting his expression of fierce concentration. 'Here it is,' he said. 'We should have another twenty-four hours at least before the real monsoon hits.'

'What's this then?' said Paulo. He was drying his feet.

'A warning shower. It will pass.'

Amber came up behind Hex and peered over his shoulder. A drip wobbled off her chin and splashed onto his hand. 'Careful!' he shouted, and snatched the palmtop away.

Amber snorted. 'A shower.' She flopped down on a bench. 'Never mind. I was going to have to come in for my shot anyway.' She took an object like a chunky pen from the leather pouch she always carried with her. Amber was a diabetic and the pen was a reusable syringe containing insulin. She set it up and injected herself. It was a ritual she had to follow twice a day, every day, and normally she would do it in private, but the others barely noticed. They just carried on talking and chatting.

However, there was a horrified gasp from the door. Sami, Bina and Radha's seven-year-old sister, was watching. She stared at Amber, her big brown eyes wide with horror, then turned and ran, shouting in Hindi.

Amber was upset. 'I didn't think anyone was watching.' She looked from Li to Hex to Paulo to Alex. She was always so careful and discreet. Now she'd scared a small child.

There were more footsteps on the veranda and Amber hurriedly tucked her equipment away. It was Bina. Sami peered round her skirts at the five friends in the house. Radha appeared behind them, her face serious.

'You know about medical stuff, right?' said Bina. It didn't look like they had come to complain.

Li asked them, 'What's wrong?'

Amber got up to make room for them on the wooden bench and plumped up the cushions. 'Come in; sit down.' Her concern showed in her voice.

The three sisters sat in a row on the bench. Bina looked worried, Radha miserable. Sami stared at Amber's abdomen, where she had seen the needle go in.

Bina asked, 'Do you know anything about

selling kidneys? I'm really worried about Mum.'

Amber swiftly sat down on the arm of the bench next to Bina. The poor girl, having something like that on her mind, she thought. 'Look,' she said, 'we'll see what we can find out. Hex—'

'Already onto it,' replied Hex. He tapped out a few commands on the keyboard. The screen reflection blinked on his face as he called up web pages, searching for information.

Fascinated, Bina and Radha went and stood behind him. For a brief while their worries were forgotten as they watched Hex use the tiny gadget to read pages from all over the world.

Hex found a site he was happy with and pointed out a paragraph to them. 'Look, it says here. *One good kidney is enough to keep the body healthy.*' He read from the screen. '*The operation to donate a kidney is a serious one but it does not shorten your life. After you have recovered you can work and participate in sports as normal.*'

Two more figures appeared at the door. Bina's parents, watching and listening.

Paulo jumped to his feet. 'Mootama, Naresh,' he

said, 'come in.' He offered Mootama the chair he had been sitting on.

'We wondered where the children had gone,' said Naresh as Mootama made herself comfortable. 'You have information about selling kidneys?'

'I've found a bit,' said Hex.

Mootama spoke in a quiet, calm voice. 'I know I will have to have tests. Can you tell me what they are?'

'Hang on,' said Hex. 'I saw something about that.' He hit the BACK key. 'Yes, here we go. *Donors' cells must match the recipient's, otherwise the recipient's body will destroy the new kidney. Living donations are usually best from people related to the recipient because the kidney is most likely to match their tissues. But it's also possible to find matches between people who aren't related at all.*' He flicked to another page. 'Ah here we are, the tests themselves. They'll take some of your blood and mix it with some of the recipient's blood in a test tube. If the cells kill each other, it's not a good match. If it is a good match, the doctors will check your general health and whether your kidneys are working well. You will have X-rays and scans, but they should not be too uncomfortable.'

Mootama was nodding as Hex spoke. 'Yes, this is what I was told.'

Li was sitting nearest to Mootama. She saw the redness around her eyes; the woman had been crying.

Naresh stood behind his wife in an attempt to comfort her. But he looked lost too. 'It is better this way. Otherwise we will have to use a moneylender. We don't want that. You use a moneylender and you spend your life in debt; you can never pay it off.'

Was he still trying to convince himself? thought Paulo.

Mootama took up the story. 'The moneylenders knew we would need to borrow. They kept offering us loans, but we told them to go away. So they said there was another way to make money. They sent the kidney man.' Her voice took on a note of pride. 'I sell my kidney, we stay out of debt. The girls get their dowries.' She stood up. 'Bina, Radha, Sami – these good people need to eat. Let's leave them.' The three children obediently rose and followed their mother to the door.

Naresh paused on the way out. 'Thank you for finding out about it for us. The kidney man, he knows many people who have sold. Some people do it to get dowries. Some of them to get out of debt. One of them bought a car and became a taxi driver. He gave us testimonials. All of them said they were all right afterwards.'

They heard the family splashing out into the wet street.

'I don't know about you,' said Li quietly, 'but I think they all look terrified.'

Alex looked at his watch. It was indeed time to eat. He poured some water into the big pot they used for rice and put it on the kerosene stove to boil.

Paulo watched the blue flames lick against the base of the pot. 'I've lost my appetite.'

Amber took charge. 'Come on, guys, we need to keep our strength up.' She dug a measuring cup into the sack of rice and measured out five portions. With her diabetes she couldn't afford to delay her meal times, no matter how unhungry she felt.

'Typical Amber,' said Hex. 'Always thinking about her stomach.' But even he sounded half-hearted.

Normally Amber would have skinned him for such a comment but her head was spinning. What if she had been born here, where people had to sell parts of their bodies to give their children a proper start in life? Someone with a condition such as diabetes would never be able to afford the drugs that she took for granted. Even if you managed to get insulin, without regular check-ups and tests – which cost money – you could go blind or lose a limb. Who knows how different her life might have been?

Alex took some vegetables from the store and silently sliced them for a curry. Meanwhile Hex was looking for more material on the web. Paulo and Li watched over his shoulder.

'This is a website for people who want donor organs. Listen.' Hex read from the screen. '*I am a fifty-year-old male in dire need of a kidney. Please help me find one. I would like to live a little longer. I would pay all expenses for donor to travel to Jerusalem.*'

'*Dios,*' said Paulo softly.

Hex flicked to a new page. 'Here's another. *I lost my left kidney to cancer, then the right one.*

For four years I have been on dialysis. The doctors have put me on the transplant list but no-one has been suitable. I am six foot five and I have to do four hours dialysis every two days. Dialysis is very painful and I cannot work or participate in normal activities. I need a new kidney as soon as possible. Donor would have to travel to me as I am too ill to go on a plane.' Hex looked up. 'He's in Texas.'

Alex cut up a tomato. 'I had no idea there were so many people needing kidney transplants.'

Hex scrolled through more web pages. His face became grimmer and grimmer. 'There are loads of them all over the world. Hearts, lungs, livers . . . So many sick people and not enough donor organs.'

Li looked out of the window at the house next door. 'Mootama is very brave.'

Hex's fingers were opening more pages. 'She might have to be braver than she thinks. It's a serious operation. She'll lose a rib. It'll take her longer to recover than it'll take the person with the new kidney.'

Alex chopped hard and fast. 'I hope that however much Mootama is getting, it's worth it.'

5
FRIENDSHIP

First thing next morning, Alpha Force headed for the building site as the sun spread pink and orange through the sky. Clouds gathered above, but they were white and benign – for now. Could they get the roof on before the weather broke?

Radha was waiting for them beside the tarpaulined walls, along with the two boys who had helped yesterday plus another brother and sister. 'Brought you some more help,' she said proudly.

'That's brilliant,' said Alex. 'We get one assistant each.' He looked at the kids. 'Who wants to help me?'

Four hands shot up, eager to be picked.

'Radha, where's Bina?' asked Li.

Radha's mouth was a tight line. 'She has to be mother now.'

The words tumbled out of Amber's mouth before she could stop them. 'You mean your mother's gone already?'

Radha nodded and turned away quickly. She was upset.

Amber regretted her tactless question. She put a hand on the girl's shoulder. 'If there's anything you or Bina need, we'll help if we can.'

Every second counted if they were to beat the rains. They ripped off the tarpaulins and got to work. Radha's friends provided a constant supply of breeze blocks and mortar, while Alpha Force did the building. In no time the walls were finished. Just as they were laying the last blocks, Pradesh the foreman – his toothache now treated – drove up with a delivery of the next materials: timbers for the roof. All hands raced to unload the truck and sort the pieces. This was the next phase, an important step.

Pradesh showed Alpha Force how to lay out the wood and position it to make four large triangle frames. Alex went over each frame, checking the many angles before hammering the pieces together, while Paulo and Hex improvised a pulley with spare wood and a rope. Amber, Li and Pradesh assembled a frame of scaffolding around the structure.

The sky darkened and a chilly wind blew over the workers on the site. All activity stopped. Faces turned up to the threatening sky. Should they rush to cover the walls?

Hex, lashing a rope around a block, glared up at the forbidding clouds. 'Don't you dare. I've got military satellites watching you and you shouldn't be here.'

The dark clouds passed and the sky brightened. Work resumed. Everyone chattered and laughed at the near miss. Paulo grinned at Hex. 'That was pretty cool.'

Hex nodded. 'Those rain clouds know who's boss,' he said, with mock solemnity.

After a couple more hours of furious work, the younger children were flagging. But they didn't want to leave. Li had a good idea – she organized them to keep all the workers supplied with fresh drinking water. Labouring in the hot sun was exhausting and their water bottles were soon depleted, so the two youngest children brought them refills from the standpipe in a large jug.

Once the triangle frames were ready, Paulo and Hex took up positions at their pulley, and told Alex, Amber and Li where to tie the ropes. Pradesh gave the command and Paulo and Hex hauled for all they were worth – and the first frame rose into the air. Paulo had designed the pulley so it could pick up the load and then swing it round, like a crane. Alex, Amber and Li guided the frame into position on top of the walls. As it settled, a great cheer went up.

The first part of the roof was on the school.

The next three went up easily. Next Paulo and Hex hoisted the crossbeams into place. Then it was up onto the scaffolding to secure them – and the roof was ready for tiling the next day. As the sun slipped down, it bathed the pale wood of the newly erected roof frame in golden light. They flung the tarpaulins up to cover it for the night. It had been a very good day's work.

Ten happy, tired youngsters gathered on the veranda of Bina's home and tucked into a supper of rice-flour pancakes with a potato curry and mustard seeds. 'Eat up,' said Naresh, nodding encouragement. 'After all your hard work, you deserve it.'

Alpha Force didn't need telling twice. Kerosene lamps cast a warm glow like a campfire. Bina moved through the guests, collecting empty plates. The kerosene light glowed through the filmy material of her sari and sparkled off the tiny mirrors sewn into the fabric. But her face was a picture of worry, furrowed with a frown that she couldn't shake off. Alex remembered the exotic creature in turquoise he'd seen on TV. The burdens of adulthood had made her look so much older now.

'How was your day, Bina?' he said as he handed her his plate.

Bina nodded. 'OK.'

Radha, sitting next to Paulo, piped up, 'It's her birthday.'

Amber gave a squeal of delight. 'Bina, is it?'

Bina looked embarrassed at the attention. 'Yes.'

Amber had a small plaited cord of red cotton around her wrist. She took it off, reached forwards and fastened it around Bina's arm. 'Friendship bracelet.'

Bina smiled shyly, and put down the stack of plates she had been collecting. She turned her wrist, admiring it. 'Thank you.'

'It looks nice on you,' said Amber.

Alex watched the two girls and remembered what Amber was like when he first met her: the spoilt, rich, bitter Amber who never noticed anyone else, let alone their problems. He got out his phone, switched it to camera mode and recorded the moment for posterity.

Bina and Amber jumped at the flash.

'You rat,' said Amber. 'I wasn't ready for my close-up.' She held out her hand. 'Let me see.'

Alex passed over the phone. Amber inspected the picture, a critical expression on her face.

'Hmm,' she said. She didn't look impressed.

Bina, though, peered at the picture in wonder, her eyes enormous.

Alex grinned. 'I'll e-mail it to you when you get computers in the school.'

At that moment a great wind blew up, licking dust up off the road in clouds. It snatched at the girls' saris, whipping them up around their faces and making them laugh in surprise. All the party leaped to their feet, grabbing plates, lamps and cushions. Suddenly the gathering was in chaos.

'Inside!' called Naresh, and they didn't need telling twice. Bina and her sisters dashed for the door. The skies opened and tipped out their rain with a heavy, metallic roar.

It was quite a crush in the little house. Hex looked out at the rain, already pouring as if through open taps from the veranda roof. 'Great. We have to walk home in this.'

The ground looked like a dark lake, the surface frosted with the constant blast of raindrops. Less fastidious than Hex, Alex leaped out into it. 'Last one in the water's a sissy.'

Paulo grabbed Li's arm and ran into the open, dragging her along. They nearly slipped over in the wet mud but recovered with a kind of skidding movement, like snowboarders doing a duet.

Amber let out a whoop of delight and leaped into the nearest puddle.

Alex looked back as they splashed across towards their own house. 'Where's Hex? The big girl's blouse – is he afraid of getting his feet wet?'

'I'll get him,' shouted Amber, waving the others on ahead. She ran back through the downpour to Naresh's veranda and peeked inside.

Hex was sitting at the little palmtop screen with Bina, Radha and Sami clustered around him. Naresh sat to one side but was listening too as Hex spoke. Amber looked at the scene. Behind her, Li and Paulo were having a mud fight. Their shrieks of delight mingled with the pounding of the rain. Inside, Hex was reading to three frightened girls.

'Look, here's a site set up by people who've donated kidneys. It says: *My mother gave a kidney so that my son could live a normal life. I owe everything to her.* Here's another: *My doctor said I needed a transplant, but the waiting list was two years. Without hesitation, my brother said, can I donate one of mine? Thanks to him, I have never been on a machine and am fit and well today. He is too.'*

Amber stepped into the open doorway. 'Your mum will be all right,' she said gently. 'And she's really helping somebody.'

6
ORGAN THIEVES

Up on the scaffold at first light, Hex, Li, Amber, Alex and Paulo could see how the rains had changed the landscape. The parched fields were turning green. The ground, previously dry as a bone, had turned to thick mud and was crisscrossed by the tracks of people, animals and vehicles. As the sun grew hotter, steam rose, obscuring the trees.

Stacks of roof tiles were laid out like packs of cards along the planks of the scaffolding. The first job of the morning had been to unload them from Pradesh's lorry. The hot sun had already dried out the timber roof-frame, so they were able to get on with nailing the tiles into position. This was the last stage that they had to complete before the rains started in earnest. Radha and her friends were hard at work too, fetching supplies. Soon the air was full of the rhythmic sound of hammering.

Below them, the day unfolded. People went out into the fields and hitched cattle to ploughs. The hairdresser arrived in a smoky diesel van and set up his chair next to the standpipe. Soon he had a queue of customers. A large grey cow wandered loose along the street, snuffling the ground for food. A thin figure in rags the colour of the mud moved around the hairdresser, picking up rubbish swept in when the ground turned into a lake. The people in the queue chatted to each other but never acknowledged him. It was as though they couldn't see him. Paulo had read about the untouchables – people in the lowest class of the caste system who did the dirty jobs such as cleaning and rubbish disposal and lived in their own part of the village. He was amazed that such otherwise friendly people could ignore the man.

Alex had a view over the other side of the village.

For a few minutes now he had been watching someone in the distance, coming towards them. The figure walked slowly, as though it carried a great burden of troubles. Now he looked up again. Recognition hit. He sat bolt upright on top of the roof ridge.

'That's Mootama!'

Everyone looked round, then at the figure who laboured slowly through the slippery mud, her skirts splattered. She looked as though she had been walking for a long time.

Radha stood up on the scaffold and let out a piercing whistle across the fields. 'Dad! Mum's back!' She gathered her skirts, clambered carefully down onto the sloppy ground and splashed towards the bedraggled figure.

Amber was sitting next to Hex. 'She's back already? I thought she'd be gone for days.'

'She should be,' said Hex. 'And she would hardly be walking. Maybe something went wrong.'

They watched in silence as Radha greeted her mother, linked her arm through Mootama's and led her towards the house.

* * *

Li needed a bigger hammer. She could see it on the ground, about four metres down. The ladder, though, was over at the other end of the building. Li decided to take the quick way down. She leaned forwards, tucked her knees into her chest, somersaulted off the rafter and landed lightly on her feet on the ground.

'Wow!' said a voice. 'Can you teach me to do that?'

Li whirled round. 'Bina! What are you doing here?'

'I've been demoted. I'm no longer mother, just plain old Bina. Is there anything I can do?'

'Yeah,' said Li. 'Come and help us at the north end – it's the last bit that needs tiling.' She steered Bina towards the ladder. 'Er – we'll take the normal way up.'

They climbed to the north end of the roof. Paulo and Amber were working there now, fixing the ridge tiles.

'How's your mum?' said Amber. 'We saw her coming back.'

Bina picked up an armful of tiles. 'She's OK. They

sent her home. She only had one kidney anyway.'

Paulo stopped hammering. 'She only had one kidney?'

'The other one was stolen.'

Her words stopped all activity: Paulo and Amber, their hammers poised to strike; Alex, bringing more nails; Li, making her way along the ridge; even Hex at the far side, collecting more tiles.

'Someone stole her kidney?' said Alex.

Bina nodded slowly. 'Years ago, she was ill. She had bad stomach pains and went to hospital. I was small at the time, but I remember she was in a lot of pain, before and after. There was this clinic funded by a charity, so we didn't have to pay. They said she had a gallstone and they had to operate. But now the doctors say her kidney was taken out as well.'

Alex was disbelieving. 'Somebody removed her kidney and she never knew?'

Bina shook her head. 'Until now. She went for the tests – all those blood tests Hex told us about. She matched and everything. So the doctors examined her and that's when they saw her scar. It goes all the way round from her back to her front, like this . . .' Bina drew a line with her index finger.

Hex and Li had come closer so they could hear. When Bina drew the scar for them, they winced. It went from the middle of her back, around the bottom of her ribcage and almost to her breast bone. They remembered what Hex had said about how the surgeons removed a rib. How painful that must be they could only imagine.

Bina wiped something away from her eye and Paulo realized she was crying. He put an arm around her. Bina sat quietly for a moment. When she next spoke her voice was quiet and angry. 'Mum was sick for months after that. She couldn't walk properly for two weeks. She couldn't lift anything. I had to fetch all the water – it was before we had the standpipe. She had to have painkillers for such a long time. We thought it was because of the stone. But it was because someone stole her kidney.'

Some movement down in the street below caught Amber's attention. A yellow vehicle, splattered with mud, was bumping over the ruts in the unmade road. 'Hey – do you often get taxis coming out this far?'

They all looked at the vehicle.

'It might be passing through,' said Hex.

But it didn't. Once it reached the standpipe, the driver braked and cut the engine. A figure got out of the back. He was overweight; that was the first thing they noticed.

'He obviously doesn't work in the fields all day,' said Amber. After a week of being among people who were lean from hard work, someone who obviously ate a lot more than he needed to fuel his body was very noticeable.

Bina had gone pale. 'That's the kidney man. What's he doing back here?'

7
TRILOK

Trilok leaned on the taxi to get his bearings. There was the standpipe, the telephone box; nearby the half-built school. As he remembered, the house he wanted was the second one, with the veranda that had the pink fabric in the doorway. Mootama's house. The fabric billowed as though somebody was beating it; little clouds of dust puffed up from underneath it. Somebody inside was sweeping the floor. Good. She was at home.

He had to think how he would handle the situation. He wasn't expected. He wondered what sort of reception he'd get. He didn't often turn up unin-vited. Usually people asked him to come to them. They'd say: *Trilok, find me a kidney. Trilok, sell my kidney.*

It was a real blow to find that Mootama had already lost a kidney. She was a perfect match for old Gopal. And Gopal was difficult because he'd rejected a kidney before. To find that this woman was such good material was a blessing indeed. And then it had all gone wrong.

As Trilok stood there collecting his thoughts, his phone rang. He took it out of his shirt pocket and glanced at the screen. Gopal again. Without even answering it, he could hear the man's rasping voice, knew what he was going to say: *Have you gone back to that woman yet? I can't hang on for ever while you start searching again. That woman matches me. End of story. You've found your donor. Do whatever you have to, but I want her.* Trilok had heard those same words many times in the short time since the doctors had examined Mootama and sent her packing.

Trilok turned his phone off. He didn't need to

hear that all over again for yet another time. He took a deep breath and made his way towards the house. Might as well get on with it. He stepped onto the veranda. The pink silk wasn't moving so much now, but he could hear the swish of the broom in another part of the room. He knocked on the wooden balustrade to announce his presence. The way he saw it, at the moment, everybody had lost out: Gopal; himself; but also Mootama, who needed money or she wouldn't have come to him. All he was trying to do was put things right.

When the man walked up to Mootama's house and knocked, Bina looked horrified.

Paulo put a hand on her arm. 'Do you want us to come down with you to see what he wants?'

She was about to answer when she saw Naresh striding in from the field. 'It's all right. Dad's going to see.' She put her head down and concentrated on counting out tiles.

Paulo and the others got the message: she was worried but she didn't want to talk. They went back to work, but they were all wondering the same thing.

Why had the kidney man come back? While they worked, they kept a careful eye on Mootama's house.

After about thirty minutes the pink sari curtain was snatched aside. Mootama stormed out. She stood on the veranda, leaning on the balustrade and taking deep breaths. Then she put her face in her hands. Her shoulders began to shake.

Amber, hammering nails into tiles, watched. Would someone else come out after Mootama, to offer comfort or to persuade her back inside? No one did. Clearly inside the house the conversation carried on with just Naresh.

She looked over at the taxi, which was still waiting. The driver had dozed off, his arm hanging down outside the window like a thick dark rope and his head lolling on his shoulder.

She looked back at Mootama. What had the kidney man said to upset her so much? And what was he saying now to Naresh? She bashed another nail in, hard.

Between hammer blows, she heard shouts. At the other end of the roof, Pradesh was shouting to the others: 'Rain. We must get down. It's too dangerous to be up here.' His next words were drowned by an immense clap of thunder, as if the sky was splitting.

Amber finished the tile she was on and made her way to the scaffold. The rain began to pelt down. She looked again at the house with the pink sari.

From their quarters, the five friends saw the portly figure of the kidney man rush out of the house, pull open the taxi door and climb in.

'Why did he bother to come back?' said Li.

'I wonder,' said Hex.

Something in his voice made everyone turn and look at him: Paulo, scrubbing at his curls with a towel, paused; Amber stopped unlacing her boots; Li, undoing her plait, paused, her fingers twined in her hair.

'I have a theory,' said Hex, 'but it's not nice.'

Paulo pulled the towel off his shoulders and hung it on the drying rail. 'Spill the beans, Hex.'

Hex sat down. 'He wants her kidney, right?'

'Yes, but he can't be trying to get her to sell her

other one,' scoffed Amber. 'She can't live without any kidneys. Don't be a dumb-ass.'

'Not such a dumb-ass,' said Hex. 'Why has he come back? Why doesn't he find a kidney somewhere else? He's come back to persuade her to sell.'

Outside, the sky was the colour of gunmetal. A thunderclap like a gunshot made them all jump.

'Hex,' said Li, 'your imagination is running away with you.'

'No,' said Hex. 'Think about it. He'd tell her it was for her daughters. A sacrifice so they had dowries and a safe future.'

'But no-one would sell their only kidney,' said Amber.

Hex looked at her gravely. 'You saw the messages on the website – people are desperate. His buyer might have told him to get that kidney or else.'

'Anyway,' said Amber, 'he went away empty-handed. We saw him leave. Mootama didn't go with him.'

Paulo said, very quietly, 'That's not necessarily the end of it. People have been murdered for less.'

A squall of rain lashed the building like white noise.

'I heard a story once,' said Li. 'A man goes abroad. He has a drink in a bar. Next thing he knows, he wakes up in the bath in his hotel room. He's got a tube in his back, he's surrounded by ice and he's had a kidney removed.'

'That's just an urban myth,' said Amber. 'Everyone's heard that one.'

'How much is myth?' said Li. 'That's almost exactly what happened to Mootama.'

'Right,' said Hex. 'And who's going to notice when a woman from a little village goes missing?'

'I agree,' said Alex quietly. 'I think Mootama is in danger. Someone may try to kidnap her. And sooner rather than later.'

'You're right,' said Paulo. 'The kidney man came back very quickly. He's under pressure. We should set up a watch tonight.'

Alex placed a kerosene lamp on the floor. 'We'll make a plan of the area. This is Mootama's house.' He hooked one of his wet socks off the drying rack and laid it flat on the floor. 'This is the road.'

Li waved her hand in front of her face. 'Phew, that's a bit smelly! Can't we use something else for the road?' She laid down her towel to represent the paddy fields.

They worked together, building up a detailed picture of the area with items to hand in the house. Every bush, every tree, even the standpipe by the main street, had been remembered and was represented on the plan. If the model was as detailed as possible, they would be better prepared.

'OK,' said Alex. 'Are we missing any details?' He sat back on his heels and looked at the village in miniature, spread out in front of him. 'What's over here?' he said, indicating the area behind the row of houses in the main street.

Li looked out of the window to check. The rain was easing, although it hadn't stopped. The sky was a little brighter. 'Just paddy fields,' she said. 'And they're under water at the moment.'

'So no one can get in from there,' said Alex. 'Or from here,' he added, indicating the other field. 'It would take too long and be too slippery.'

'And you certainly couldn't take anybody through it if you were kidnapping them,' said Hex.

'Thank heavens for the monsoon,' said Amber. 'It looks as though the only way in or out is the road.'

Paulo put a couple of spice jars down on the model. 'If we have two people at this end, where the houses peter out, and three people at the other, we've got the whole village covered.'

'And we don't have to get too close to Mootama and the girls,' said Alex. 'They're probably scared enough already.'

Hex was on the palmtop, consulting the weather satellites. 'We'll have a clear night,' he said. 'The next rains aren't due until tomorrow.'

Sure enough, outside the rain was stopping.

'Here's what we'll do,' said Alex. 'We'll go out now and finish the tiling, and have a look at our laying-up points while it's still light. At dusk we'll take up our positions.'

8
KIDNAP WATCH

The night air was hot. The fuggy smell of swamp water from the paddy fields mingled with the fragrance of jasmine and mosquito repellent. Hex, Amber and Alex were at one end of the village; Paulo and Li were at the other.

At each end the routine was the same. They settled into the shadow of a large, solid tree, and waited. They wore camouflage cream on their faces, hands and necks so that they couldn't be spotted in vehicle headlights.

But once they had settled, all they had to do was wait.

Surveillance was a tedious, tiring business. They had to keep as silent and still as possible to blend in with the surroundings. They had to stay alert for hours on end, looking into the blackness, listening to the night sounds. At first there was plenty to do as they had to become accustomed to their environment. The wildlife seemed to be constantly on the move. A troupe of baboons passed, chittering to each other, their paws pattering on the wet ground. A cow wandered past, its hooves heavy and slow. Further out in the dark, monkeys hooted, chickens squawked, antelopes and deer skittered away from wild dogs. Occasionally they heard a train or a lone vehicle in the distance.

For a while it was fun to identify each noise, but once they had been there for an hour, they had heard all the night repertoire. Now, unless an intruder came, it would be the same for hour upon hour. They started a sleep rota. If something happened, the alert one would wake the other and they would tackle it together.

Being on watch was tough. It was easy to succumb to boredom, to lose alertness, perhaps even fall asleep. This is where their discipline and training came in; it helped them to remain focused in spite of the tedium.

Hex got out his mobile. Every half-hour the two different watches would send each other a text message. That way they could keep in contact and check that everything was still normal. His thumbs typed away. 'IS IT A BIRD?' he wrote to Paulo. 'IS IT A PLANE?'

Immediately he got an answering bleep: 'IS THAT BEST U CAN DO AFTER HALF AN HR? NO PLANES HERE. BIRDS AND BABOONS.'

Hex put his mobile away. Everything was normal, then. He shifted position and sighed. Amber and Alex were asleep beside him. They dozed sitting up, their backs to the tree.

Then Hex heard a noise in the bushes. He stiffened, listening. He tuned out the rhythmic breathing of his companions. No, it wasn't one of the usual noises.

He leaned over to Amber and Alex and tapped

them on the shoulder. They awoke instantly and without a sound. They were trained to become alert straight away, without making any noises that would betray them.

They all listened, holding their breath.

Amber heard it first. 'Something coming this way.'

'It'll be a wild dog or something,' said Alex. They had already had several alarms. Small animals seemed to be in the habit of detouring through the bushes in the ditch by the road.

Hex relaxed. 'It's in those bushes again.' Maybe it was a dog.

They heard the noise again.

'This sounds big,' said Amber.

'I'll go closer,' said Hex. 'You stay here.'

He picked up a long stick and moved away from the road, prodding the path in front of him and pausing with each step. It would be easy to step on a snake.

There was definitely something rustling in the bushes. Something large. A cow? Then it moved again and he saw a faint outline.

It was human.

'Contact!' yelled Hex. He gave chase. 'Stop!' he called, pulling out his torch and switching it on. A figure was crashing through the bushes, fast, but he couldn't see anything distinct. It was shadow on shadow.

Alex caught up and stopped him. 'It's all right, they're going away,' he panted. 'Let them go. The main thing is that we scared them off.'

Hex breathed hard, flashing the torch after the intruder – whoever it was, the figure was too far away to be distinct. His heart was hammering, adrenaline surging through his veins, demanding action. 'Do you think that was him? We should have chased him.'

'No we shouldn't,' said Alex. 'What would you do with him if you caught him?'

Hex realized what was in his mind. 'Give him a good beating.'

'Exactly. And we're not here to do that, even though he might deserve it. We're just here to keep him away.'

They walked back to Amber. She had stayed at

the checkpoint in case an intruder decided to slip in while Alex and Hex were diverted.

She had her mobile out, her thumbs typing a message. 'I'll tell the others we've seen someone.'

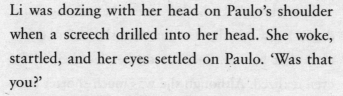

9
GONE

Li was dozing with her head on Paulo's shoulder when a screech drilled into her head. She woke, startled, and her eyes settled on Paulo. 'Was that you?'

Paulo's head was bent over his phone as he texted the others. 'It was you,' he said. 'You were having a nightmare.'

For just a microsecond she believed him. Then she saw three chickens clucking away down the road, heads up, fleshy combs wobbling. One of them squawked again. There was the real source of the noise. The dawn chorus was starting. She cuffed Paulo lightly around the ear.

The sky was growing pale. Peacocks shrieked from their night-time roosts. Monkeys hooted in reply. The sun was nearly up, already bringing its scorching heat to the day.

Paulo sent a message: 'VISIBILITY GOOD. STOP PATROL?'

He got his answer in a few moments. 'YES. RACE U 2 BREAKFAST.'

He jumped to his feet and grabbed Li. 'Come on,' he said, and took off at a run.

Even though Li hadn't seen the message and didn't know why he was running, she wasn't going to be left behind. She was on her feet before she even realized. Although she was much shorter than the big South American, she was very fast and she quickly caught up with him.

She and Paulo ran side by side down the main street, past a clutch of tiny houses set aside for the untouchables, past children pattering onto verandas and women in colourful saris setting off with brass containers for the standpipe.

Alex had already reached the house. Amber and Hex splashed in just as Li and Paulo appeared from the other direction. They all lunged for the veranda and touched the balustrade, as if touching a base at the end of a race, and fell against it laughing.

'Alex,' gasped Amber, 'you had a head start.'

'He didn't,' retorted Hex, getting his breath. 'You were just too busy fixing your hair.'

Amber was about to answer when they heard a shout: 'Bina?' Something about it made them all take notice.

Mootama was standing outside her house, looking up and down the street. She called out again, more loudly, 'Bina! Where are you?'

Alex walked over to her. 'Mootama, what's the matter?'

Mootama's face showed she feared the worst. 'Bina is not inside. She is not out here fetching water. I have looked everywhere. She is gone.'

Alex pulled the others into the house for a conference. 'No one came in last night,' he said quietly but emphatically.

'What about that intruder you scared off?' said Paulo.

'He never got in,' said Hex.

'What if someone reached the house?' said Li.

'Impossible,' said Alex. 'They couldn't walk through the fields. And nobody could get into the house without waking everyone up.'

'We'll search for her,' said Alex. 'Maybe she's gone for a walk.' But somehow he doubted it.

'I think a good place to look would be where you had the contact,' said Paulo. 'There are bound to be some tracks.'

'Tracking is your domain, Alex,' said Li. 'Why don't I take Amber and Hex to where Paulo and I were positioned and we'll work our way back from there looking for clues.'

Alex squatted on the ground in the ditch. He had been shown by an aboriginal in Australia how to spot tracks, and how to tell what – or who – had made them. But the ditch wasn't telling any stories. It was thick with branches and twigs. Some had been squashed into the mud where they had been trodden on, but there were no prints visible.

He straightened up and looked along the gulley. Whoever it was went that way, he thought.

Paulo was a little further up the road. 'How about this?' He waved a prickly branch at Alex. On it was a scrap of dark blue cloth.

'It looks like it's from one of those shawls the women wear,' said Alex. 'Probably a villager.' He peered more closely.

Paulo looked at it. 'Walking in the ditch?' Then it came to him. 'You know your contact? You thought you'd stopped someone coming into the village – but what if they weren't coming in but going out?'

Alex thought. 'But it was only one person; he didn't have Bina with him.'

'What if it was Bina? On her own?'

Alex shook his head slowly as he digested Paulo's words. In his mind's eye he saw the turquoise creature picking her way through the paddy field, the mirrors on her sari catching the light. 'No, that's not Bina's. Her saris have got all those twinkly bits.'

Paulo gave him a look. 'If you were trying to get

away in the middle of the night, would you wear twinkly bits?'

'I wouldn't wear them anyway, mate,' said Alex, 'but you please yourself.' He became serious as Paulo's words struck home. 'But you mean . . .'

'I mean, it was Bina you saw. She went along the ditch so she wouldn't be seen, with her sari covered up. She went out to meet the kidney man.'

Alex nodded slowly. Of course. He turned and began to stride down the road alongside the ditch. His thoughts were churning. It had to be Bina they saw; it made sense. If he'd let Hex catch her . . .

But there was no time to be angry with himself. They were bound to come to tracks soon and if he didn't concentrate he might miss them. The mistake had been made; if he spent too much time punishing himself he might make another and that would help no one. He pushed the recriminations to the back of his mind.

Soon Alex's vigilance paid off. A set of footprints appeared on the road. He turned to Paulo. 'Here she is.'

They squatted down to look more closely. 'There

are some others here too,' said Paulo. 'These were made about the same time.'

'A man in sandals,' said Alex. 'The footprints face hers as though she stopped and talked to him.' He walked a little further, bent double, looking at the ground intently. 'Paulo!' he called.

He pointed at the ground. The footprints had gone haywire, scuffling and skidding. They were crossed by a line of tyre tracks. 'What does this look like to you?'

Paulo looked at the prints. 'I'd say there's been a struggle. While they were getting her into the car. She didn't want to go.'

Alex nodded. The regrets came flooding back. If only he'd let Hex get on with it. He took out his mobile and texted Amber: 'FOUND TRACKS. BINA TAKEN. RV @ HSE.'

She texted back: 'WANT ME 2 TELL M?'

Alex replied: 'YES.' Then he felt like a coward. If anyone broke the news, it should be him; he was responsible for the mess. Then he thought, No, Amber's on the scene. It'll take us a while to get back. When we do, we need to ask some questions.

The sooner Mootama is able to answer them, the sooner we can go and get Bina back.

But he sent another text to Amber: 'THANX.'

Paulo followed the tyre marks to the edge of the grass. He got on his hands and knees to look at them more closely. 'Perhaps I can see what kind of car—'

Suddenly a cobra rose out of the grass. It spread its hood and let out a vicious sound like a high-pressure air hose.

Alex realized Paulo had stopped talking rather abruptly. He turned and saw the snake, its head swaying above Paulo's, the hood wide open like wings. The hair stood straight up on the back of his neck. He couldn't move.

Paulo could see every scale on the snake's body. He didn't even dare to breathe. He closed his eyes and moved back very, very slowly.

When he opened them again, the snake was subsiding back into the pale grass. Paulo got to his feet shakily and moved further away. Sweat was running in cold rivulets down his forehead and inside his shirt.

Alex clapped him on the shoulder. 'I think somebody doesn't want you to look at the tyre tracks.'

'Well, tough, I did,' said Paulo. 'It was a saloon car. Rather like the taxi we saw earlier. Now, I wonder who's been visiting here in a taxi?'

10
PRISONER

'I've got her in the clinic, but I'm having to keep her doped. And we may have trouble.' Trilok hooked the phone under his shoulder while he grappled with his breakfast, a dosa – a large crispy rice pancake – bought from a stall. He tore a piece off and put it in his mouth.

'Trouble?' said the voice at the other end.

Trilok swallowed. 'When I went to see the family there were these western kids nosing about. They're aid workers or something. You know what they can be like. They have no idea about our way of life but they think they can interfere.' He walked across a stretch of grass, past a sign saying that the park and the white, domed building behind it had been constructed in 1913. He picked his usual bench and sat down.

'Don't worry, Trilok. I'll be on the lookout.' There was a pause. 'Enjoy your breakfast.'

Trilok cut the call. The past twelve hours had been exhausting. Finally, things seemed to be going in the right direction. He'd spent a gruelling afternoon talking to Mootama and Naresh, patiently explaining that all was not lost. All they had to do, he said, was send someone in Mootama's place. Did she have a sister, a brother? Another blood relative? He didn't mention the children but the couple understood. They'd been upset; Naresh had shouted at him. But Trilok had expected that. He was used to it. He had continued, patiently, to explain how the deal could still be done, they could still earn the money; $700 – 32,000 rupees – could still be theirs, if they could send somebody who would be the same tissue type as Mootama. Think of your daughters, he told them. This will be their dowries.

Of course, the price Gopal was actually paying Trilok for the kidney was $8000 – 365,000 rupees. And today he felt like he'd earned it.

He'd almost been back in Chennai when he got the call. It was from a number he didn't recognize. He said hello cautiously; you never knew who could be calling or why. A hesitant voice replied: young, female and nervous. Probably it had never used a phone before. 'This is Bina from Nayla,' it said. 'I want to earn my dowry.'

He told her to meet him just outside the village. No point in turning up in the taxi to find the parents waiting for him with sticks.

When she turned up she'd looked so young he almost sent her back home again. She had big eyes like a frightened animal, and was wearing a dark shawl thing so she wouldn't be seen. But the really young donors did get scared sometimes. He'd seen it before. 'Come on,' he said. 'We'll take you to the clinic and get your tests done.'

That was a mistake. It spooked her. He tried a different tack. 'There's a nice bed waiting for you

– clean sheets – lots of friends, too.' That usually worked.

That was when she said: 'I don't want to go right away. I just wanted to talk about it first.'

He'd got hold of her arm by now; good thing too or she might have run away there and then. He tried reasoning with her. 'What is there to talk about? Think of your sisters, your dowry.'

But the silly girl had panicked. She had put up quite a fight before he'd got her into the cab and given her something to calm her down.

Trilok finished his breakfast and wiped his fingers on a tissue. He'd still got her drugged, but the important thing was that he'd got her. And he wasn't going to let her go.

11
ON THE TRAIL

Mootama sat in the big rocking chair, her knees pulled up to her chest. She looked much older than her thirty years; worry had etched lines into her face and her eyes were red with crying. But now she was calm. She felt comforted talking to the teenagers; they were not very much older than Bina, but they seemed so grown-up, so in control.

The two girls had broken the news to her – that it looked as though Bina had gone to meet the kidney man but had been taken against her will. The boy who had the little computer had said they would try to find her, as though it was the kind of thing they did all the time and it would be easy. Then the other two boys had come back and the questions started in earnest.

'I was taken to a clinic,' said Mootama. 'There were lots of people there with kidney trouble – on machines, or waiting for tests, or seeing doctors. There was a house behind the clinic, through a locked door. I was taken there and told that was where I would live. There were other women there who were selling kidneys. They were very friendly. It was nice and clean, although there were bars on the windows. I was told the tests would take forty-eight hours, then the operation could be done. But as soon as they saw I'd already had a kidney removed, they threw me out.'

'Do you know who was going to have your kidney?' said Amber.

'He was a rich man who'd had a transplant before. It had gone bad. He wanted another from a live donor because they last longer than transplants from dead people.'

Mootama got up. She went through to the kitchen

and began to sort through the washing up in the sink. Even though her daughter had gone, there was still the rest of the family to look after.

Hex said: 'I wonder if the client is holding her?'

Alex was shaking his head. 'No. She's no good to him there. She'll be having tests. If we turn up at the clinic I bet she'll be there.'

'Mootama, can you tell us where the clinic was?' asked Li.

Mootama sighed. 'I don't know Chennai. I've never been there before. They drove me in the taxi. When I left, they gave me the bus fare and I didn't take in where I was – I just wanted to get home as soon as possible. I couldn't find my way back there.'

'You wouldn't need to go there again,' said Amber. 'We'll go. If you come too somebody might recognize you and hide Bina.'

Li asked, 'Did you notice anything about the neighbourhood once you were there? The name of a shop . . . ?'

Mootama had a turquoise shawl in her hands. She looked at it for a long moment, thinking. Alex recognized it as Bina's. That little voice spoke up inside him: *You should have let Hex stop her.* He forced it down and pressed Mootama gently for an answer: 'Anything you can tell us will help us find the clinic. Anything . . .'

After a long moment, Mootama nodded. 'Yes, I looked out of the barred window of the room I shared with the other women. There was a cinema, and next to it, a chemist's.'

'A cinema, great,' said Hex. He took his palmtop out of its carrying case. 'There can't be many cinemas in Chennai. Let's see where they are.' In no time he had a list. 'OK, there are nine cinemas in Chennai. Mootama, can you remember what film was showing?'

Mootama thought and then shook her head.

'No worries,' said Hex. 'I've got a list here. Have a look and see if you recognize any.' He handed her the palmtop, the screen facing towards her.

She shook her head and handed it straight back. 'Bad eyes. You read them.'

Hex took the palmtop back from her and looked at the list. And swallowed. The first title was *Kucch Rishtey Kachche Dhaagon Ke*. If he tried to get his tongue around that he'd never be understood, and Mootama might be insulted by his attempt. He looked further down: *Kuthu*; *Lakshya* – they weren't too bad. *Aparichithan* – getting worse. Then *Kyunki Saas Bhi Kabhi Bahu Thi*.

Amber peered at the screen. 'So come on, tell us what's on.'

Hex deleted the link before she could get a good look. His fingers raced over the keys, looking for another site. 'Aha!' He waited for the screen to finish loading and took it to Mootama. He had found a site that included graphics of the posters for each film. 'Just nod when you want to see the next one.'

Mootama looked at the screen over his shoulder, her brow furrowed in concentration. Hex cursored to the next poster, and the next. Then she nodded. 'This one. *Aparichithan*.'

'And that, my friends,' said Hex, 'is showing at the Regal in Victoria Road. Next question: how do we get there?'

Paulo looked at his watch. 'Pradesh is going to be here any minute now with fixtures and fittings for the school, and he said he'd have to go into

Chennai for more. If we help him unload in double-quick time, we can hitch a ride into town.'

Alpha Force didn't need telling twice. In an instant, they were on their feet and heading for the door. Mootama looked a little bewildered at the sudden activity.

Li put her hand on the woman's shoulder. 'We'll find her, don't worry. We'll bring her back safe and sound.' Mootama nodded. Then Li followed the others outside.

They made their way towards Pradesh's truck, which was pulling to a halt next to the building site. 'Mootama said the tests take forty-eight hours.'

'So that's our deadline,' said Paulo.

'Probably less,' said Alex. 'She went in the middle of the night.'

Hex looked at Alex pointedly. 'Did she?'

Alex met his eye. 'Yeah. I mucked up. I should have let you catch her.'

12
CHENNAI

'Hey, nerdboy,' said Amber, 'look at the real world.'

Hex looked up from his palmtop and out of the window. When they set off, it was down a rough road between the flooded paddy fields. On each side men ploughed the water with teams of black buffaloes. Small villages nestled between the meadows. Now, barely thirty kilometres away, they were on a wide tarmac carriageway. The fields had turned into a sprawl of buildings stuccoed with peeling plaster the colour of ice cream and stained from years of monsoon.

'Yuck,' said Hex. 'And it's still muddy.' Amber gave him a look of scorn. He smiled inwardly at how easy she was to wind up. Then he retreated back into his thoughts, idly flicking through websites. But he was only half paying attention even to that. He was mulling over what Alex had said about the previous night and re-running the scene in his head. The indistinct figure in the torchlight, its outline broken up by the bushes. It hadn't occurred to him that it might be Bina. He'd been about to catch up with her too, when Alex had stopped him.

But he couldn't blame Alex. What they did had made sense at the time. Now they'd have to put it right.

Pradesh put the brakes on, hard. The van screeched to a halt.

'What's happened?' said Li.

'Cow in the road,' said Pradesh, 'so everyone has to go around it.'

The large grey cow was lying peacefully across two lanes. The orderly lines of cars, bikes and lorries became a chaotic scrum as they tried to pass it on either side. In the middle of it all the beast lay calmly, its jaw rotating thoughtfully as it chewed, unperturbed by the squealing tyres and honking horns.

'You'd think it would be scared of the traffic,' said Alex, 'but it's just sitting there.' A bike roared past the beast, just inches from its nose. The cow didn't budge.

'That's cows for you,' chuckled Paulo. 'You can't move them when they get comfortable.'

'How will its owner get it out?' asked Amber.

'Its owner probably set it free,' said Pradesh. 'Food is scarce, but the cow is holy so no one will kill one. That is why their owners let them wander into the cities.'

Hex reached into a holdall on the floor and brought out a small black pouch. He passed it to Amber. 'Take one and pass it on.'

She reached inside. Her fingers pulled out a small silver locket on a leather thong. She smiled, recognizing it like an old friend. Li was next, and recognized hers too. They were miniature transmitters to allow Hex to track the team in the busy streets of Chennai.

Hex, Alex and Paulo had similar devices, on small rings like washers. They fitted the washers over the hooks of their belt buckles, under the leather.

'Quick check,' said Hex, and pressed a button on the palmtop. The display showed a map and a cluster of pulsing dots. 'Yes, all working.' He powered it off again.

Outside, the landscape had changed again. The smell hit them first: a greasy mixture of drains, dung and diesel fumes. Gradually, as they reached the town centre, the buildings became closer together and taller, the advertisement hoardings more frequent. They were in the heart of the city.

'Sure this is the one?' Alex looked up at the massive Art Deco facade of the Regal Cinema. It was painted in red and blue and displayed a huge cut-out of Marilyn Monroe. Pradesh's truck disappeared into the traffic.

Hex pointed to the pink and yellow poster advertising the movie *Aparichithan*. 'Yes, that's it. And there's the chemist's shop two doors along.'

'Then that looks like the place we want,' said Li.

Opposite the cinema was a long, low, single-storey building painted in pale yellow. The sign said: ST THOMAS'S CLINIC. One section of the building had bars on the windows.

Li turned round and pretended to take an interest in the film poster. 'How are we going to enquire about her?'

Amber joined her. 'We could say her mother is ill and asking for her to come home.'

'Risky,' said Alex. 'That might really worry Bina if she heard us.'

'Suppose we say we're her friends and we've come to visit her,' said Paulo. 'Nothing suspicious about that. And we'll just see what they say.'

'I'll go in,' said Li.

'And me,' said Paulo.

'Right, that means Hex, Amber and me are back-up,' said Alex. It was their standard practice when investigating to go in twos. Then, if they had to follow up or try a different approach, there were still three who hadn't been identified. 'We'll find an RV point and text you the location.'

* * *

In the clinic's reception area, a fan rotated slowly below a yellow ceiling. A nurse holding a clipboard bustled up to the counter. 'Yes?'

'A friend of ours is here having treatment,' said Paulo. 'She asked us to bring something for her.' He patted the small leather bag on his belt pack as though it contained the item. In reality it contained a toolkit.

The nurse frowned. 'What's her name?'

'Bina Bhattacharya.'

The nurse shook her head. 'I don't think we've got anyone of that name here. What was she in for?'

Li thought quickly. The principle was always to say as little as possible, and to stay as close to the truth as possible. 'Tests, I think.' She deliberately made it sound vague. The less they seemed to know, the better. 'But she definitely said it was here.'

Paulo's phone bleeped: he had a message. He clicked to open it. It was from Amber. A photo of Bina came up on the screen; it had been taken a few days before at the building site. She was standing next to Li and Paulo, holding a trowel.

'Look,' said Paulo. He showed the picture to the nurse. 'Here's what she looks like.'

The nurse stared at the picture. Her manner changed. 'No,' she said sharply. 'Your friend is not here. She has not been here.'

The same thought occurred to Li and Paulo simultaneously: Why had the nurse's mood changed? But they were careful not to let their reaction show in their faces.

The nurse gave the phone back to Paulo, keeping it at arm's length, as though looking at the picture was going to make her give something away. 'You'll have to go now,' she said. 'If you don't have an appointment you can't see anybody.' She turned away from the desk, as though eager to escape.

Definitely trying to hide something, thought Paulo. And flustered by it; as though she doesn't have to do it very often. But it was clear they weren't going to get any further by asking questions.

He pulled Li's sleeve. 'We'd better go,' he said. He looked at the nurse. 'Sorry to have bothered you.'

They turned and left the clinic. Beside the

entrance, a rubbish bag was propped against the wall. A rat scurried away as they approached, but it had left a hole in the black plastic. Something caught Li's eye and she crouched down as though tying her shoelace.

She only needed a glance. In among the papers and wrappers that had been thrown away was a small red band of plaited cotton. It was Amber's friendship bracelet – the one she had given to Bina. What was it doing there?

13
CONSPIRACY

'Has Alex texted the RV?' said Paulo.

Li clicked through her messages as she walked away from the building. 'Yes,' she said. 'South for a couple of blocks; the park with the big white building.'

The route took them back past the gaudy cinema. They walked slowly, like two friends having a chat. Someone might be watching from the clinic, so they wanted to look as casual as possible.

They reached their first turning. 'There's someone behind us,' said Paulo. 'He's been there since we came out of the clinic.'

Li kept her voice quiet. 'Do you think he's

following?' They kept walking at the same unhurried pace.

'Might be.'

They went past a café with a big smeared window. They paused and glanced in, pretending to read the menu but using the glass as a mirror. They could see him, three metres behind them – a man in a dark red shirt and fawn linen trousers.

'He didn't stop when we stopped,' said Li.

'That doesn't mean he's not following,' said Paulo.

'I might be being paranoid,' said Li, 'but I think we should lose him before we meet the others. We mustn't bust their cover.'

'Let's go round the block here,' said Paulo.

They turned down the road. Li took out her phone and pretended to make a call, but she was using the polished screen as a rear-view mirror. The red-shirted man turned too. 'He's still behind.'

Paulo chose another turning and Li watched in the screen. The man carried straight on. 'We've lost him. All clear.'

Paulo grinned at her. 'Just paranoia. We've been doing this job too long.'

Li shook her head. 'That nurse looked paranoid enough to do anything. If I were her I'd have tailed us.' She hit a speed-dial key and called Alex. 'No joy. They say they don't know her, but they're hiding something, big time. Before we left we saw a friend-ship bracelet thrown in the bin – it looked like Bina's. I think we should go to the police, get them looking for her. There's something fishy going on at that clinic.'

'We'll see you at the police station,' said Alex.

'I want to report a kidnapping,' said Alex. Alpha Force stood in the reception area of the police station – a poky corridor bounded on one side by a long counter. A floor-mounted fan stirred a faint breeze that fluttered the notices yellowing on the notice board. At the end of the corridor a tiny woman dressed in rags was lugging along a huge bucket of water and a mop.

An officer stood behind the counter, shuffling papers. His khaki uniform showed dark flowers of sweat under each arm. He carried on shuffling as Alex spoke – until he heard the word 'kidnapping'.

'You want to report a missing person?'

'Yes,' said Alex. 'She's—'

'Wait, please. I fetch Sergeant Chopra. He looks after missing persons.' The man disappeared through an arched doorway.

A minute later another officer came through. Unlike his colleague he obviously wasn't confined to desk work. With his khaki uniform he wore a gun belt and holster in leather the colour of ox blood. But whatever he did, it couldn't have been very active: a large paunch protruded over his waistband like a balloon. Not for the first time, the five friends couldn't help but notice the contrast with the lean villagers.

Sergeant Chopra spoke. 'You want to report a missing person.'

Paulo gave a brief description. 'She's just turned thirteen years old – went missing last night from the village of Nayla—' He got no further.

'Nayla? That's not in our district.'

Li leaned on the counter and looked at him earnestly. 'We have strong reasons to believe she's been brought here. We think she's been kidnapped to steal her kidneys.'

Sergeant Chopra turned his back on her before she had finished. Li looked at his solid bulk disbelievingly.

He turned round again and put some papers on the desk. 'Start by filling in these forms. We need your names, addresses, address of your parents or guardians, relationship to the missing girl . . .' He spread the forms out in a fan shape. There were several pages to each.

Li looked at the paperwork with mounting incredulity.

Alex knew that expression; soon it would change to impatience. Li wasn't the most diplomatic person in the world. He stepped in. 'We'll give you all the details we can. Can I borrow a pen?'

Li spotted a biro beside the telephone. 'There's one.' The policeman picked it up, slowly took the cap off and handed it over. Then he disappeared through the door again. Li glared at his sweat-marked back.

Alex took charge of the form and they filled it in. A short time later the sergeant returned. 'Have you finished?'

Alex handed the papers over in a neat pile. The sergeant put them straight into a basket on the desk.

'What will happen now?' said Alex.

Sergeant Chopra folded his hands in front of him on the counter. He looked like a Buddha. 'We'll look into it.'

Li butted in. 'There's somewhere you could look right now. We think she's here in Chennai. We saw something belonging to her at St Thomas's Clinic – a friendship bracelet we gave to her. We think that's where she is.'

Sergeant Chopra maintained his implacable pose. 'We'll get someone onto it,' he said. 'Thank you. You can go now.'

The five friends were all dying to talk, but they made sure they were well away and out of earshot before they let rip.

Hex got his comment in first. 'Ever had the feeling that someone wasn't very interested?'

Li practically exploded. 'He didn't even look at the forms we filled in.'

'Do you know what else is odd?' said Alex. 'He never asked if we had a picture of her.'

'That's right!' added Amber. 'I was just about to show him the picture and then I got this hunch. I thought I'd wait and see if he asked for it. Don't you think there was something really odd about him? He gave me the creeps.'

Paulo was a little more laid back. 'Maybe that's just the way they operate in this country.'

Li snorted. 'Perhaps we interrupted his morning nap, but if we don't find Bina fast, someone else is going to be operating.'

Alpha Force weren't the only people who didn't want to be overheard. Sergeant Chopra watched them disappear, had a quick look around the station to make sure no one else was nearby, then got out his mobile and pressed a speed-dial key.

The phone was answered briskly. 'Yes?' It was the kind of 'yes' that says the speaker already knows who the caller is.

'Trilok,' said the sergeant, 'you'll have to move the girl.'

14
UNDERCOVER

'We have to go back to the clinic,' said Li. 'Bina's friendship bracelet was in the bin outside, and yet they're denying they've seen her. Paulo and I have already been there, so it'll have to be one of you guys.'

They sat in a large formal garden – Alex's original RV point. Behind them a big domed building gleamed like a white meringue in the sun.

Paulo was lying on his back, eyes closed. He looked as if he was asleep, but he was thinking as hard as anyone else. 'We need to get further than reception. There's nothing there. We need to really search the place; go where Mootama went.'

'They've got those bars on the windows,' said Alex. 'That's going to make a covert approach tricky.'

'And I bet there are alarms too,' added Hex. He was lying on his side, looking at the manicured grass and picking out stray long bits the mower had missed.

'Why don't we take the bull by the horns?' said Amber. 'Ask if we can see someone about selling a kidney? They might show us around.'

'Whoa, whoa.' Hex put his hands up to stop the runaway thought before it became too bizarre. 'Reality check: only poor villagers sell kidneys. None of us look remotely like one of those.'

'Good point,' said Alex. 'No matter what we do we'll look like tourists. Although there are quite a lot of those around.'

'I've got it!' said Amber. 'Backpackers. They're all over the place. We could be backpackers in trouble – run out of money or something.'

Alex nodded slowly. 'That sounds good.'

'Better if it's just one backpacker on their own,' said Hex. 'Stranded or robbed after months of travelling. And therefore desperate.'

The others murmured in agreement.

Paulo spoke without even opening his eyes. 'So which of us will make the most convincing backpacker?'

Li prodded him. 'Now who might pass for a lazy oaf who fell asleep and lost his wallet? If it wasn't for the fact we've already been identified, I'd say it had to be you.'

Paulo grinned. He started to croon the old Frank Sinatra song, echoing her words back to her.

The others put their hands over their ears and groaned loudly.

'Eek, stop!' protested Amber.

Paulo opened his eyes. 'I'm sorry,' he said. 'I was singing in my sleep.'

'I vote we send him to donate his organs,' said Li. 'All of them.'

Amber leaned down and unzipped what looked like a pocket in the thigh of her black trousers. The whole leg came off, turning them into shorts. She had been wearing long trousers out of respect for the villagers and to keep mosquitoes away, but the backpackers they had seen wore shorts and T-shirts. '*Voilà*,' said Amber. 'And since I'm American the clinic won't connect me with you and Li.' She unzipped the other leg, then folded both of them into a pocket in the back of the trousers.

'What about the backpack?' said Li.

Hex took off the small rucksack he'd brought their tracers in and held it out. 'A backpack.'

'That's not big enough.' Amber curled her lip. 'It's supposed to carry all my worldly goods. That wouldn't even carry my make-up.'

'Say your main one is in the left luggage at the station,' said Hex. 'This is your shopping gear.'

'Or better still,' said Alex, 'you left it there and it's been stolen. You've lost everything and that's why you need to sell a kidney.'

Amber slipped the backpack onto her shoulders.

Paulo sat up. He looked at her critically. 'It still isn't enough. You need more gear. You should look like a beast of burden.'

She put her hand on her insulin kit. 'I've got this too.'

He unclipped his toolkit from his belt and handed it to her. 'You can't have too many bits and pieces. That should look like a money belt.'

'She's not supposed to have any money,' said Hex.

'Well, act like it hasn't got money in it,' said Alex. 'Put it on, Amber.'

Amber took her belt off, threaded the toolkit onto it and fastened it again.

The others nodded. 'Yeah, that looks better,' said Li.

Amber knew how much the kit meant to Paulo. He had made many of the tools himself. 'Thanks, Paulo,' she said. 'I'll take good care of it.' She eyed Hex's palmtop in its belt-mounted carrying case and a big grin spread across her face. 'Perhaps I need another—'

Hex's hand immediately flew to his most treasured possession. 'Forget it!' he said firmly. 'You're not having that.'

Amber hit him gently on the shoulder. 'Keep your hair on. I was only asking.'

'See if they can give you a personality transplant while you're in there,' rejoined Hex.

Meanwhile, Alex had been working out a plan. 'Amber, you go in, have a good look around the clinic and the safe house behind it. That's your priority. I'll be your backup. I'll wait outside, across the road. Check in every half hour. If I don't hear from you, I'll get Hex to dial up your tracer and we'll come looking. OK?'

Amber nodded.

Hex grinned at her. 'Of course, they might surgically remove it.'

'Gee,' said Amber, 'you really know how to keep up morale in a nasty situation.'

15
THE CLINIC

Amber was nervous; her blood was pounding like her heart wanted to jump into her throat. She waited in the yellow-painted reception of the clinic, under the fan that turned slowly in the yellow ceiling. On the counter was a list of services the clinic offered, like a menu in a hotel. Perhaps reading it would keep her calm: dialysis from 1,700 rupees; blood tests 100 rupees per test; dialysis plus tests 2,500 rupees; assessment for transplant by arrangement.

It made her feel even more as though she was venturing into the lion's den.

Stay objective, she told herself. What do we notice from this? The clinic specializes in kidney disease. And there were no prices listed for an actual transplant.

A nurse came out and addressed her briskly. 'Yes?'

Amber opened her mouth, began to speak, and shut it again. She'd thought she would have to pretend to be a bit nervous, not her usual confident self. But she actually was quite scared. She was going to invite these people to buy her kidney and they were going to take her seriously. Knives and scalpels flashed in her mind's eye like warnings. She wanted to turn round and leave. She swallowed and began to speak again. 'I wonder if I could have a quiet word?'

'What about?'

Amber swallowed. She had no trouble making it sound as though she had come to a difficult decision. Her voice was almost a whisper. She couldn't have spoken louder if she'd tried. 'I've been backpacking for four months and I've run out of money. I can't get home.' She bowed her head. The nurse leaned closer to hear. Amber had to force herself to say the words. 'I heard there are people who need kidneys. Do you know who I could talk to about helping them?'

The nurse straightened up. Her expression was flinty. Oh my God, Amber thought. She's not falling for it. It's illegal, isn't it? She's going to call the police. I'll be arrested.

But the nurse said, 'Have a seat through there.' She indicated a doorway separated from the reception area by a row of hanging strips of plastic, like ribbons.

Amber went through. Well, that was the first hurdle. But she didn't feel triumphant; she felt sick.

As she walked through the ribbon curtain, she saw a woman sitting on a plastic chair, reading a newspaper. The woman glanced briefly at Amber, then turned back to her paper. She looked very tired.

Amber remembered how she used to feel before her diabetes was diagnosed: tired and listless; unable to concentrate. It was horrible, not being well. It made you an unhappy, unfriendly person. Along with that memory came another warning: diabetes could lead to major diseases; a likely one was kidney failure. This could be a glimpse into the future. If Amber had been nervous before, she now felt as though someone had shaken her hard.

She forced herself to think positive. *I'm fine*, she said to herself. *I'm going to look after myself and stay healthy. Now*, she went on firmly, *do your job*.

The rest of the room was divided up by hospital screens. One was not quite closed, and Amber managed to glimpse a man lying on a bed, tubes going into his arms and snaking under his shirt; the other ends of the tubes fed into a tall machine. It was then that Amber became aware that there was a noise in the room, louder than the sound of the traffic outside and the fan beating overhead. It was a sort of liquid gurgle. It must be the sound of blood circulating through a dialysis machine.

A nurse came through and looked at the woman on the chair. 'Mrs Chaudhuri,' she said, 'this way, please.' The woman got up stiffly and followed the nurse to one of the trolleys. She levered herself onto it slowly and lay down.

The nurse took some needles out of a wrapping and lifted the woman's shirt.

Amber looked away. She wasn't squeamish about needles; far from it as she had to inject herself twice a day. But this was a private moment she shouldn't see. Then the nurse remembered to close the screens.

There was a door opposite where Amber was sitting. It had a numerical keypad: a security lock. Whatever they had in there, they wanted to keep people out. What had Mootama said? She was taken through a locked door into another part of the clinic. Well, there it was.

Another nurse bustled through from reception and approached the door. She pressed five keys, opened it, went through and made sure it closed behind her.

From her seat Amber counted the number of keys on the pad – numbers 0 to 9, plus the letters A to D. That made fourteen keys – and over half a million possible five-figure combinations. Too many to guess.

Someone else sat down beside her. Amber remained wrapped in her own thoughts until a voice broke through.

'You're new. You don't look ill like me. You can't be coming for dialysis.'

Amber turned round. She had a shock when she saw her new companion. The voice was male but at first glance Amber could have sworn it was a woman; a heavily pregnant woman. His entire belly was swollen, from the chest downwards. Thin arms and legs poked out from his sleeves and trousers like sticks. His face was greyish under the brown skin, the eyes sunken.

'Today is my day for dialysis,' he said. 'That's why I look like this. If you had seen me earlier in the week I would have been smaller. Everything I drink, all the water I take in, it stays in my body because my kidneys don't work any more. Are you here for tests?'

Amber nodded.

'Good,' said the man. 'That is better than being ill. I used to be well.'

Amber felt like a fraud. How could she pretend she was going to sell a kidney when the people who needed them were this ill? She should walk out of there right now and not deceive him any longer. But he seemed to want to talk to her, so she said the only thing she could. 'Where will you get a new kidney?'

'There's an agent who is looking for a donor.'

The man would probably tell her so many things that would be useful. But squeezing him for information seemed callous. *Do your job*, she had to tell herself. *You might not find anyone else to ask. It's for Bina.*

She took a deep breath. 'I would like to talk to the agent. Do you know where I can find him?' She couldn't meet his eyes as she asked the question, in case she saw a flare of hope.

'He visits the clinic. I don't call him, he comes and finds me when he has a possible donor.' The man shrugged. 'After all, he knows where to find me.'

'What happens then?'

'I pay him!' The words came out as a brittle laugh. 'He has to have the donor tested and that costs money. My illness has made me a poor man.'

Amber sat in silence, unable to think of anything to say.

The man sighed. 'I was an engineer. Now I can't work. I've sold everything my family owns. I have to pay for dialysis. I have to pay for tests. I need dialysis twice a week but because I am paying for tests I can't afford two lots of dialysis. It is like a gamble. Every tiniest test costs money but it is like an investment; there is hope in them. Dialysis is just standing still.'

'How long have you been waiting for a donor?'

'Two years. All the doctors say I'm too ill for a transplant. They won't look for donors for me. But the agent will. He will help me when no one else can. And whoever gives their kidney, they will be doing a wonderful thing.' He looked directly at Amber. His brown eyes were surrounded by yellowed whites. It was a direct appeal from a dying man: *Heal me.*

The nurse finished tending to the woman on the dialysis machine and beckoned to the man. He tried to get up but staggered, unbalanced by his distended belly. Amber stood up and put out her hand to help him.

'Thank you,' he said, 'but I can manage.' He walked stiffly towards his machine.

Amber sat down again to wait. She was shocked. She had to say to herself: *He's not the man who's expecting Bina's kidney. So by rescuing Bina you're not depriving him of life. Remember you are here to help someone. And sometimes you have to see some hard things in order to do that.*

The nurse hooked the man up to his machine, pulled the screen around him and bustled out of the room.

Amber realized no one had come to see her for a while. Had she been forgotten? Perhaps the staff were busy. Still, the longer they delayed, the more she could find out. If she could bear it.

She had to get through that locked door, but how? She got up and glanced over at the figures at the machines to see if they noticed, or cared. No, they were off in their own private worlds. Was there anything in Paulo's toolkit that she could use? She opened the zip and peeked inside. There seemed to be a lot of probes, screwdrivers and nut-and-bolt type things. She frowned. How could anyone need that many? But anyway, what good would they be against the numerical lock? She zipped the bag up again.

Amber walked up to the door and looked closely.

If the lock was used a lot, she should at least be able to work out which keys were used more than the others. That would narrow down the possible combinations to about 120. Hmm, she thought, still not brilliant.

A noise alerted her from one of the trolleys. She looked round. The engineer was beckoning to her. His screen was slightly open. She didn't want to go over. Those jaundiced eyes made her feel like a fraud.

'Two-four-seven-C-B – and hold down the seven while you do the C,' he said. 'I've spent hours lying here with nothing else to do and I've worked it out.'

Amber gave him her widest grin. 'Thanks,' she said and skipped over to the door. *Put him out of your mind*, she told herself. She punched in the combination and slipped through.

16
THE DONOR

Something odd was happening outside the clinic. Alex saw it mirrored in the screen of his phone. He was outside the cinema, pretending to key in a text. There had been a few comings and goings: he had seen the swollen man walk stiffly in, leaning back to balance his huge belly. But now a youth was holding onto the railing at the entrance, shouting at someone in the doorway of the clinic. He was much younger than most of the patients who came and went – more like Alex's age; certainly not the usual age of someone needing kidney treatment. Of course, it wasn't impossible, but Alex thought it was odd.

The boy turned and leaned heavily on the railing along the walkway. Then very slowly he made his way back to the road. Was he drugged – or in pain? Something about him made Alex's spine tingle.

The boy was so wrapped up in his misery he didn't notice Alex cross the road, heading straight for him. When Alex nearly bumped into him, it looked like the most normal thing in the world.

'Sorry,' said Alex.

'Sorry,' mumbled the kid.

When Alex got a good look at the boy's face he was shocked. His skin was slick with sweat and his eyes were half closed.

'Can I help?' said Alex. 'Are you all right?'

'They won't take me,' said the kid. Alex now noticed his breathing was shallow and fast. Definitely in pain. And shivering, despite the clammy heat.

'Who won't?' said Alex. There was a bench a little way along the road. It was also out of sight of the clinic – he was trying not to be spotted in case he had to go in later. 'Here,' he said, and took the boy's arm. 'Come and sit down.'

The boy took tiny, painful steps, leaning on Alex. When they reached the bench he lowered himself down very carefully, just like Alex's father had when he had broken some ribs on an exercise. A rib? Mootama had lost a rib when she had her kidney stolen. Had this boy just sold a kidney? Or, worse, had one stolen?

'You said they won't take you,' said Alex. '*Who* won't take you?'

'The clinic. Now they've got what they wanted.' The boy spoke through clenched teeth.

Got what they wanted. Should he ask outright? The boy might get scared or turn violent. On the other hand, he didn't look capable of much. Alex decided to chance it. 'They took your kidney?'

The boy nodded.

'Here, in this clinic?'

'No. They sent me to a hospital.'

'When?'

'Six days ago. They threw me out.'

'What do you mean, they threw you out?'

'The man who bought my kidney. He was feeling better. He didn't want to pay for me to stay in hospital any longer. He came to me and said, *I feel better so you must too*. But I'm still in pain. He could walk; I couldn't. I told him, *I'm still in pain. I'm cold all the time*. He said, *Here's your money, now get out. If you try to stay I'll get the police*. I didn't dare stay.'

So the transplants weren't done in the clinic; they were done in a hospital. Perhaps Bina would be taken there. This was an important lead. 'Where is the hospital?'

The boy shook his head violently. 'No. They will call the police if I go back there and I will go to prison . . .' His voice started to rise in panic.

Alex swiftly changed the subject. 'You got your money?'

'Yes.'

'So you could go to another hospital. I'll help you get there.'

The boy shook his head vigorously. 'No. The hospitals will know what I've done and arrest me. So I stay here. The clinic will have to take me. They kept me safe before.' He shuddered violently, as if he was trying to keep warm.

Alex put a hand to the boy's forehead. He had a fever. He probably had a post-operative infection. He needed antibiotics – and some good painkillers. No wonder he couldn't think straight. He could go to a private hospital and get treatment, but he thought everyone was watching him. And, Alex realized, I'm probably not helping by questioning him.

'Listen,' he said. 'I want to help. Why didn't the clinic let you in?'

'They said they couldn't treat me. Said I should be in hospital. I said I can't stay in hospital. They said they couldn't treat me there. But they'll have to take me back.'

Alex was sure they wouldn't. The clinic were probably terrified to see a donor coming back, especially in that state. What would new donors think if they saw him?

Was that what would happen to Bina too? Would she be carved up and broken like this? Mootama had taken months to recover when her kidney was taken.

'Listen,' said Alex, 'I want to help you. If you tell

me where this other hospital is, then I'll know where I shouldn't take you.' Somehow, he had to get the name.

The boy started to hyperventilate. 'No,' he said. 'Don't take me back there. They will put me in prison.'

'I won't take you there, I promise.'

'I stay here,' said the boy stubbornly. 'They have beds, medicines, nurses in the clinic. They will have to take me eventually.'

They were going round in circles. The boy was nearly delirious and fixating on this one idea. Did he really think that if he sat on this bench for a few hours, the clinic would take him back? And how would Alex persuade him to tell him the name of the hospital? If he didn't, this could well be what Bina would look like in a few days' time.

The kid got up. 'I'm going back to the clinic now.' Alex went to stop him. They'd only throw him out again.

But the kid never got that far. He stopped and leaned against a lamppost, barely twenty metres away, panting as though he had been running hard.

Alex went up to him. He looked worse. Alex put his arm around the boy to steer him back to the bench.

The boy screamed.

Alex pulled away, shocked. He'd never heard anyone scream like that. 'Sorry,' he said. 'Sorry.' He took him by the arm instead.

The boy could hardly walk now. How could he have deteriorated so fast? Alex wondered. Should he leave him where he was? No, surely he would be better sitting down. Very slowly, he led the boy back to the bench and helped him settle. The boy lowered himself awkwardly, as though he couldn't bend in the middle. He needed help, and quickly.

Alex's hand was wet. He wasn't surprised; the boy was drenched in sweat. He took a tissue out of his pocket to wipe it and suddenly saw that his hand was red. Blood.

A big red stain was seeping slowly through the sodden yellow material of the boy's shirt. It was where the operation wound would be.

Alex went cold. When the kid had tried to go back to the clinic, the wound must have ruptured.

Should he lift the shirt and have a look? It didn't seem to be bleeding fast; the blood was seeping out slowly. If he moved the shirt he might make it worse. But one thing was clear: he had to get help now. If that wound opened any more the boy might bleed to death.

A plan rapidly formed in his head. He'd have to leave the kid for a while. He didn't want to, but if the boy heard what he was going to do he would still stubbornly refuse.

Alex made his voice reassuring. 'OK, just stay here; don't go anywhere. I'm going to go and talk to the clinic. Make them help you.'

A little light of hope shone in the boy's eyes. It wrenched Alex's heart strings. I hope this will work, he thought. 'Promise me you won't move from here until I get back?' he said.

The boy nodded. Alex glanced at the wound again. No more blood had come out, but there was no time to lose.

Alex jogged away towards the clinic but stopped just round the corner. He took out his phone and dialled as he went.

The call was answered. 'Independent Aid Inc.' It was a western voice, a little sergeant-majorish in tone.

Alex began talking quickly. 'I'm with the school-building programme in Nayla. I'm in Chennai with one of the villagers and he urgently needs a doctor. Can you help?'

'We have doctors but we can't let just anyone see them.' The voice was reproachful, like a teacher telling him off.

Alex froze. 'I beg your pardon?'

The answer came in that same reprimanding tone. 'A lot of people on programmes get attached to the villagers, but we make it our policy not to interfere. Otherwise we'd be treating half of India.'

This was the last thing Alex had expected. He wanted to just scream, *This is a young kid in trouble!* But he took a deep breath. He remembered his dad's anecdotes about dealing with difficult officials. *Listen to all their rules and objections*, he'd said, *and look like you're taking them seriously. And don't rush them.* 'Oh, I see,' said Alex. 'Under what conditions do you help with medical treatment?'

'Like I said,' said the voice, 'we can't find medical treatment for everyone. Our doctors cost money.'

It took all Alex's patience not to lose his temper. How did aid programmes end up employing bureaucrats who didn't want to help people? It made his blood boil. He glanced round the hedge. The boy hadn't moved, but he might have passed out. If he fell off that bench the wound might split wide open and then . . . Alex shuddered.

He took a deep breath. 'No, of course you can't treat everyone.' He tried to sound as though he had all the time in the world. 'But for future reference, so I don't make this mistake again, can you tell me when you will?'

'We can only give medical treatment to staff who are registered on the programme.'

Alex seized the opportunity. 'He is! He's the foreman's son.'

'Oh, well, why didn't you say? You said you were in Nayla? Let me get my list. What's his name?'

His name? Did Pradesh have a son? Did they even know? He'd have to bluff. 'I don't know. We called them both Pradesh.'

'He must have had another name.'

Alex had to think quickly. 'Yes, but it's Indian and I couldn't remember it. So I called them both Pradesh.' He cringed; the excuse was blatantly insulting and showed the kind of attitude Alex deplored. But he couldn't think of anything else.

Suddenly there was a smile in the voice. 'Know what you mean. Some of the names are hard to tell apart, aren't they? You'll get to tell the difference if you stay here a while.'

Alex thought that if he ever met the officious, loathsome man face to face, he'd give him a piece of his mind. Northumberland style.

'You bring him in and we'll treat him.' The man gave an address and rang off.

A cab was going past. Alex stopped it and asked the driver to pull over by the bench. He saw that the boy was still conscious, but he was breathing fast. Had he got worse?

Alex knelt down beside him. The boy looked at him with wary eyes. The slash of blood across his shirt looked a little bigger – or was that Alex's imagination?

'I spoke to the clinic,' he told the boy. 'They misunderstood and they're very sorry. They have somewhere they can look after you and would like to send you there now in this taxi. I will tell the driver where to go but you're in control. You can stop it any time you want, and even get out if you change your mind.'

At last the boy seemed to trust him. Perhaps it was just because he was so ill. He nodded.

'If anyone asks,' said Alex, 'your name is Pradesh and your father is a builder from Nayla.'

Very carefully, after giving instructions to the taxi driver, Alex helped him up off the bench. Ever so slowly, the boy climbed into the cab. He settled uncomfortably, lying across the back seat, breathing hard.

'Just one more thing,' said Alex. 'The clinic want to know which hospital treated you so badly. They won't use it again.' It was a gamble; would it work?

Perhaps the boy believed him; perhaps the fight was just draining out of him and he'd have told him anyway. He said in a quiet, rasping voice: 'St Francis.'

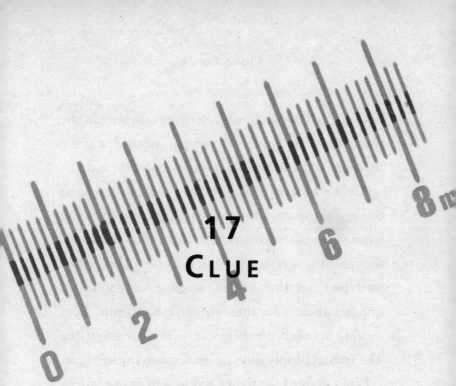

17
CLUE

'I thought I was fanatical about recycling,' said Li, 'but this is surreal.'

She was exploring the market with Hex and Paulo. Old clothes, used cooking utensils encrusted with grime, plastic margarine containers, plastic bottles creased from multiple use were on sale alongside sari fabrics and food. Between the big stalls, people were selling their wares from windowsills. A man stood in the locked doorway of an apartment building, shouting vigorously to invite shoppers to examine his collection of old drugs in battered packets. It was sensory overload: the shouting, the smell of people packed closely together and the heavy fug of spicy fried food.

Paulo's mobile trilled. As he hooked the phone out of his top pocket, a scrawny, filthy brown hand loomed up out of the crowd. For a moment Paulo thought it was trying to grab the phone, but it just stretched out like a plea, hoping for coins. An untouchable. The three friends had seen them moving between the shoppers, looking for tourists. The Indian people didn't even seem to notice them.

Paulo dodged the figure and looked at the caller's number. It wasn't Amber or Alex. The untouchable moved on to an American couple who seemed prepared to pay him more attention.

Paulo answered the phone. 'Hello?'

A hesitant voice spoke at the other end. 'Hello?' It was high and female. Young and female. The hairs stood up on the back of Paulo's neck. 'Bina, is that you?'

Li heard him and gripped Hex's arm. Hex looked at her, startled.

With all the yelling and the noise of frying food,

Paulo could hardly make out the quiet voice. 'I can't hear you!' he shouted. 'Hang on. I'll go somewhere quiet.'

He began to run through the crowd, still talking. 'Hang on. Don't go away.'

Li and Hex hurried behind him. Had Bina called?

The street ended in a park. Across a large expanse of green was the white domed building. The open space was like a breath of fresh air.

At last Paulo could hear. 'Hello?' he said.

Li and Hex stared into his face. They heard the tinny crackle of talking at the other end.

Paulo's shoulders sank. 'Yes, it's me. Hello, Radha. How are you?'

Li sighed. Hex looked down. For a moment they had both been full of hope. But maybe Radha had news.

Paulo was talking and shaking his head. 'No, Radha, not yet. But we're doing our best.' He flopped down on the grass. Then he straightened up again, listening intently. After a few moments he said, 'Radha, that's excellent. Can you read the number to me?' He gestured to the others, making a wiggling motion with his hand. He wanted a pen and paper.

Hex patted his pockets; he didn't have a pen. Li didn't either. She switched on her phone and handed it to Paulo. He keyed in the number and read it back to Radha to confirm it. 'That's really helpful,' he said. 'Well done, and tell Sami well done too.'

Li and Hex clearly heard a girlish giggle at the other end of the phone. They looked at one another. Obviously Paulo had made a hit there.

'You all be careful now,' said Paulo. '*Adios.*' He cut the connection.

'Well?' said Li and Hex in unison.

'The moneylender was back in the village, scouting for business. Sami went through his stuff while he wasn't looking. She found a card. It had a name on it: Tagore Trilok. She says it's the kidney man. And,' added Paulo proudly, 'she just gave me his mobile number.'

'So what do we do?' said Li. 'Phone him?'

Hex's fingers were already flying. 'Pass it over here. We don't need to phone him, we can do something far more clever. Mobiles work by getting a signal from cells – transmitters that send signals out in a small area. And since it's all controlled by computer . . . if we find out what cells he's been using, we can find out where he is.'

'And where he is—' began Li.

'– Bina might be,' finished Paulo.

'Exactly,' said Hex. He tapped Trilok's number into a website. First he had to find out which phone company he used. No problem. This website would identify it in seconds. He got his reply. From that he knew which website to hack into to track where Trilok was. The website asked for a password. Not a problem. He flipped open another window and accessed a program he kept for just that purpose. In moments, an answer sprang onto the screen. 'Yes!' said Hex out loud, and fired the result into the keyboard. A new screen came up. Hex scanned it briefly. A broad smile spread across his features. 'Well, well, well.' He turned slowly to the others. 'Ladies and gentlemen, in the last twenty-four hours he used his phone only in Nayla and Chennai.'

'And he's probably not far from here right now,' said Hex.

Li looked at the screen. 'How accurate is it?'

Hex looked disbelieving. 'It's dead accurate. It's a computer.'

'No, I mean, how detailed?'

'We can narrow it down to a few blocks.'

'Well, where is he now?'

'I can't see right now. But as soon as he makes or receives a call, we'll see which cells he's using. And that will tell us where he is.'

Li said, 'Let's call him. What are we waiting for?'

Paulo shook his head. 'No, I don't think we should. He'll see the number's unfamiliar. He might get spooked.'

'Can we listen to what he's saying?' said Li.

'Not without bugging equipment,' said Hex. 'But we don't need to do anything fancy like that. He's been making and receiving a lot of calls recently. It won't be long before he pops up again.'

Paulo thumped the grass emphatically. 'And when he does we can follow him straight to Bina. I bet he's not letting her out of his sight.'

'Hang on a minute,' said Li. 'We can't go running after him. We'll stick out like sore thumbs. Me, tiny and oriental; you enormous and Argentinian, Hex . . .' She looked at Hex as if thinking of a way to sum up his appearance.

Hex looked back at her. 'Yes?' he said sweetly.

'I see what you're saying,' said Paulo. 'We don't look like anyone round here.'

'Plus,' said Li, 'if he was in the clinic when we went there, or he's been told what we look like . . .'

'So that leaves me,' said Hex. 'The indefinable.' He gave Li a pointed look.

'I'm working on it,' she replied.

'Anyway,' said Hex, 'I hate to sound like a wuss, but this site is going to ask for passwords every ten minutes so I have to nurse the connection. I can't run around after Trilok.'

'Indefinable . . .' Paulo was tapping his fingers slowly on the ground, as he often did when he was thinking. 'Untouchable . . .'

Hex snorted. 'Thanks.'

'No,' said Paulo. 'Untouchable . . .' He pointed to the people flowing through the market stalls. An untouchable squatted down at the corner, watching for tourists. 'Look at him. Nobody sees him.

Nobody even looks at him. I bet if one of us dresses up as an untouchable, nobody will even notice us. We can be invisible.'

'Brilliant, Sherlock,' said Hex. 'Where are you going to get your outfit?'

Paulo looked at Li. 'Shall we do some more shopping?'

'We'll get a map too,' said Li. 'We must be very familiar with the streets. The moment Trilok's mobile becomes active, we need to know where to find him.'

18
TESTS

Amber was in a corridor. It was empty, but there were voices at the other end. She passed a bathroom, then a room with easy chairs and a television. She went in and switched it on: the noise would help cover any sounds she made as she moved around. There were bars on the windows, just as Mootama had described. It was definitely the safe house.

Was Bina here?

Amber came to a closed door. She listened. All quiet. Did she dare go in? Taking a deep breath, she turned the handle and pushed the door.

It was a dormitory: six beds were arranged along the wall. A man lay on one of them, reading. He looked up at Amber.

Amber had to bluff it out, pretend she was meant to be there. After all, there would hardly be intruders with that security lock on the door. 'Sorry. Wrong room.'

'Women's room is next door,' he said.

'Thank you.' Amber retreated quickly.

The next room was another bathroom and then there was one more room at the end. No medical facilities, then; it was just residential. All the testing must be done out in the clinic. As Amber approached the room at the end she heard laughter. Female laughter.

She opened the door. Four faces looked round at her. Amber scanned them briefly, but none of them was Bina.

They were all older – mid-twenties to mid-thirties – and skinny like the people from Nayla. Villagers who were selling their kidneys.

'Come in, dear,' said a woman in an orange sari

with curly pink patterns. 'No need to hide. Come and join us.'

'Oh, how lovely,' said a woman in an emerald-green sari. 'A young one!' She looked at her companions. 'Isn't she a lovely girl?' She patted the bed next to where she was sitting.

Amber felt herself blush. She wasn't used to effusive behaviour. Her parents hadn't been like that and it just made her uncomfortable. But she went and sat down, and called up the photo of Bina on her mobile.

'I'm looking for my friend. Have you seen her?' She passed the phone to the woman next to her, who wore a splendid sari with red and navy patterns.

'Her friend's in here too!' exclaimed the emerald woman.

Amber's heart leaped. 'Have you seen her?'

The woman in the red sari was shaking her head. 'No, dear, I haven't. But I was having my tests this morning, so I may have missed her.' She handed the phone to the next woman, in the orange sari.

'Lovely girl. No, I haven't seen her, and I've been here since yesterday.'

She passed the phone to the next woman, the one

in emerald green, who looked at the picture and handed it back to Amber. 'She's very pretty, your friend. Who could forget if they'd seen her!' The woman looked intently into her eyes. 'Don't worry. We will be your friends while you're here!'

Amber realized they thought she was asking about Bina because she was apprehensive and wanted moral support.

'Oh yes,' said the woman in red. 'We'll look after you until your friend arrives!' The emerald woman's enthusiasm seemed to be catching.

'It's lovely in here,' said the woman in orange, looking at Amber earnestly. It seemed her arrival had unleashed an outburst of mothering instinct. 'I am being taken good care of. They will only operate if I can afford to lose a kidney. You have no need to worry.'

'I wish I had done this years ago!' chuckled the woman in emerald green. 'They bring us our meals. We don't have to do any cleaning. I haven't had to fetch water. There is electricity in every room and a television. I wish I had three kidneys to sell!'

There was more laughter. Amber could hardly believe these women were preparing for a major operation. The atmosphere was more like a sleep-over party. Had they been drugged so that they wouldn't feel anxious? It would be easy to slip them some Valium to make them easygoing and co-operative. At least they weren't hugging her; Indians generally weren't very touchy-feely, so she would probably be safe.

'And don't worry about your friend,' said the woman in orange. 'She may already have gone to the hospital. In which case it's all good news because soon she will have her money!'

Amber didn't find this comforting at all, but she believed them when they said they hadn't seen Bina. They had no reason to hide anything. They were here to sell a kidney and go.

A nurse put her head round the door. 'Oh there you are, Amber.' She sounded irritated. 'Have they shown you into here already? We've been looking for you. If you come with me, we're ready to do your tests now.'

'Go on, girl,' said the woman in the emerald sari. 'You'll be fine. It's nothing to be afraid of.'

'We'll see you later,' said the woman in orange.

They waved at her, smiling broadly as she left.

The nurse led Amber out into the corridor. 'They shouldn't have shown you in here yet. You're supposed to have tests first.'

'Sorry,' said Amber. She had nothing to be sorry about, but hoped that if she sounded contrite, the nurse wouldn't ask who had shown her in.

As they passed the common room and the bath-room, Amber had a quick look in each. Both rooms were empty. That settled it. She had looked every-where in the safe house and clinic and Bina wasn't there.

The nurse took Amber back through the security door, through the dialysis room, and into another room that looked out onto a scruffy yard at the back of the building. There were no bars on the windows; indeed, this window was wide open, although it didn't seem to help the ventilation. Bina couldn't be on the premises – they would certainly have kept her in the section of the building that had bars.

The room looked like a doctor's surgery, with the usual equipment Amber was used to from her check-ups in the US. A blood pressure monitor sat on the desk alongside a stethoscope; there was a trolley with sterilized instruments, a yellow box for used needles.

'Sit down on that couch,' said the nurse. Amber did as she was told.

The nurse went over to the trolley and Amber heard wrappers being torn open. She saw a needle being fitted onto the end of a syringe.

'What are you going to do?' said Amber.

'We'll start by taking your blood. This will tell us which of the patients on our transplant list you match.'

Automatically Amber put out her left arm. And then she remembered what the man on the dialysis machine had told her. He had had test after test, paying every time, in the hope of finding somebody who was a match. What if they found she was a match for him? To disappoint him would be so cruel. Or she might match someone else. Even if she matched no one, someone would pay for this test. Someone who couldn't afford another wasted result.

The nurse came towards her, the needle glinting in her hand. 'I'll have to take quite a bit as there are a number of people to test you against . . .'

Amber saw the syringe. It was huge. She stood up and put on an expression of panic. 'No.'

The nurse glared at her. 'It's only a needle. You're not scared, are you?'

For a moment Amber found the situation funny. Thank goodness she hadn't told any of them she was a diabetic. They'd never believe that someone who had to inject herself had a phobia about them. 'If you don't mind,' said Amber, 'I need to think about it . . .' She made to move towards the door.

The nurse blocked her way. 'Just sit down and it will all be over.'

Amber backed away towards the window.

The nurse advanced, more angry now. 'I said, *sit down*!'

Amber's hands touched the sill. In a flash she had vaulted out. She landed on hard earth, rolled to her feet and was already running. There was an iron gate leading onto the street. The nurse put her head through the window and shouted something, but Amber sprinted for the gate and was out in moments. She leaned against the wall getting her breath, and called Alex.

19
CRUEL CITY

On the edge of the road, next to the park, a tattered figure sat hunched like a shivering animal. He wore stained, striped rags that looked like an old set of pyjamas. His face was greasy and stained and his head was swathed in a filthy turban. People going into and out of the park stepped over him without noticing.

Li and Hex were looking at him, though. It was Paulo. Once they'd bought some rags, he'd got into his costume immediately. Now he sat on the pavement begging, while they sat on the parched grass in the park, enjoying a snack of bhajis. Li had just taken an update call from Alex. They'd been excited about his lead but they all agreed they couldn't pin all their hopes on Bina being there. So Hex kept watching for Trilok's next phone call.

'Why is it,' said Hex, 'that Paulo makes such a good rancid, stinking old devil?' On a previous mission in Ecuador he had had to impersonate a street urchin, and had done it so convincingly even his friends were fooled.

Li shook her head. 'Maybe this is what he's like when he's out with the cowboys on the range. We're just seeing the real Paulo.'

Hex whistled through his teeth. 'The guy must have no sense of smell. And to think you found someone actually selling those old things. They probably can't believe their luck.'

Li grimaced. 'It looked like somebody had died in them.'

'Hey,' said Hex urgently. 'Our man's gone live.' He touched a key on his palmtop. 'Yes, there he is.' He leaned over the map that Li had spread out on the ground. 'Right here. Two streets away.'

He and Li were immediately on their feet, walking towards Paulo.

Paulo saw them approach. This was the signal. As they got close, he heard Li say 'Mount Road' to Hex. Neither she nor Hex looked down at him as they walked past. They were minimizing the amount of contact between them. It was very unlikely anyone linked to Trilok was watching but it would be stupid to take a risk.

Paulo got up. He had studied the map and committed it to memory. Like a cabbie, he now knew the quickest route to all the local streets. He had to catch up with Trilok immediately, as he wouldn't get any more clues. If Trilok was in a rickshaw or a car, he might be away in seconds.

Mount Road was three minutes' walk away. Paulo shuffled along to a long, dank-looking alleyway. When he was sure no one was looking, he sprinted like the wind. Li had made him swap his trainers for a scrappy pair of sandals and they weren't easy to run in. They flapped noisily with each footfall, the sound echoing off the narrow walls. A gutter ran along one edge and smells wafted out of doorways, none of them pleasant. Paulo concentrated on the light at the other end of the alley.

A silhouette stepped out of one of the doorways. It stood like a menacing black shadow against the oblong of daylight, a knife in one hand.

Dios, thought Paulo. He stopped and sized up the guy. The clothes weren't much better than the ones Paulo was wearing. Well, that explained why he was prepared to rob an untouchable.

The man came towards Paulo and babbled at him in Hindi. His teeth were large and glinted like broken stones in the light that slanted into the alley. The knife gleamed dully.

Paulo reached inside his robe and brought out his wallet.

The man stared at it and snatched it from Paulo's hand. He probably thought Paulo had stolen it himself. He flipped it open. Inside was Paulo's ID, with his photo. The man looked at it, glanced at Paulo and then back at the photo of the clean, grinning Paulo. His mouth dropped open.

Paulo seized the moment. He kicked out at the man's wrist, sending the knife straight up in the air.

The weapon came down and both of them grabbed for it. Paulo found himself holding it by the handle. His assailant opened his hand in surprise and found a gash of blood across the palm, sliced by the blade.

Paulo's wallet was on the ground. He grabbed it and ran for the oblong of light.

He emerged, the blood surging in his ears like thunder. This was Mount Road. *Focus*, he told himself. *Where was Trilok?* He might have gone by now. How long had that little detour taken? Maybe it was seconds. It felt like an hour.

He still had the knife in his hand; he chucked it over a wall.

Then he spotted Trilok. Having seen him in the village, he wasn't likely to forget him. The kidney man was leaning against the wall of an apartment block, talking into his phone. Paulo squatted down on the pavement like the beggars he had seen, and waited. One foot stirred up a cloud of flies and he felt slime between his toes. He had stepped in a cow pat. Oh well – that would only make the disguise more authentic.

Trilok finished his call and snapped the phone

shut. He set off at an amble through the streets. Paulo got to his feet and followed slowly. He met Hex and Li coming out of a side street, and walked past without acknowledging them. He knew they were tracking him anyway.

Paulo had never seen the kidney man's face this close before. The man had big, fleshy features and wore a frown. Was that the face of a man worrying about a little Indian girl he was holding captive? Anyway, he wasn't going to let him out of his sight.

On the other side of town, Alex and Amber reached St Francis's Hospital. It was modern, recently built, with palm trees in the forecourt that waved in the breeze as ambulances pulled up.

'This is where that boy had his kidney taken out?' said Amber.

Alex nodded. 'It's a lot more swish than I was expecting.'

A long limousine drew up and stopped outside the entrance. A uniformed chauffeur got out of the driver's seat and opened the back door. A figure climbed out carefully, brushing the creases out of a linen suit. On his wrist was a large gold watch. He straightened up and began to walk slowly towards the doors.

Amber remembered the women in the safe house; the patients at the clinic. She muttered to Alex, 'It looks like the clientele's a bit different here from downtown.'

Alex looked at the people going in and out of the hospital, visiting friends, bringing people for treatment. It was shocking to see people who were so well dressed after the poverty they had witnessed. It was like a different country.

'Do you really think they've got Bina prisoner here?' said Amber.

'Only one way to find out,' said Alex. 'We've got to get in.'

Amber put her hand on his shoulder to stop him. 'If we're not going to be thrown out straight away, we'd better look like we're respectable.' She glanced at the knife on Alex's waistband. Wearing it was as natural to him as wearing a watch was to other people. She knelt on the ground and opened Hex's rucksack. 'Put that in here.'

Alex handed the knife over and Amber stowed it in the bag. He still didn't look quite right. Her fingers closed around something and she pulled it out. 'Well, well, what have we here?' She smiled in delight. 'Hex uses hair gel.'

Alex looked horrified. 'He doesn't.'

Amber showed him the jar. 'Well, it's his bag and this sure as hell ain't mine.'

'The wuss,' said Alex. 'Wait till I see him.' As he turned round Amber stood up and slopped a dollop of gel onto his fringe. 'Hey—'

She silenced him with a furious look and started working the gel into his hair. 'The more groomed you look, the richer you look.'

'I *was* groomed.'

'In a Geordie sort of way.' Amber stroked the gel through his hair and sculpted it into trendy spikes.

Alex pulled a face. 'It smells like perfume.'

'Nearly done.' Amber made one last adjustment and put the gel back in Hex's rucksack. 'Ooh, here's Paulo's pink shirt—'

'No!' barked Alex.

Amber grinned. 'Only kidding. Ready?'

Alex glared at her. She might as well have tied a bow in his hair. 'I feel like a girl,' he said. 'Come on.'

Trilok moved slowly along the street. He was in another section of the market that was devoted to food. Samosas were tossed in boiling oil next to big shaking cabinets of kulfi, the condensed milk ice cream. Trilok stopped and bought a fresh mango juice. He chatted to the stallholder as he drank it.

Paulo stopped too. Some people went past him and he put his hand out, eyes pleading. They stepped round him as though they were avoiding a lamppost. Nearby was another untouchable, squatting on his haunches by a bin, watching and waiting to see what people threw away.

Trilok was on the move again. He put his hand in his pocket and took out some change. As he passed the bin he picked out something from among the coins and threw it in the bin. Then he went on to a melon stall.

The untouchable sprang up to see what Trilok had dropped into the bin but Paulo moved faster.

It had looked like a piece of paper. He had to get it. He plunged his hands in. The stench that rose up was like being punched: the bin was filled with vegetable peelings and fruit skins, fermenting in the oven-like heat of the day. Flies billowed up in an angry, buzzing cloud.

The beggar yammered at Paulo in fury, trying to keep him off his territory. Paulo was tempted to leave him to it; his stomach was heaving. As the untouchable tried to fend him off, their struggles drove the piece of paper deeper into the slimy mess. Paulo glanced at Trilok. The kidney man was standing eating a slice of melon. At least this fight was good cover; everyone had turned away in disgust.

Suddenly a massive, snuffling grey shape loomed up behind Paulo. A wide muzzle dipped into the mess like a spade and pushed it around. A cow had decided it wanted a snack. It twisted its head, trying to reach the bottom of the bin. Its horns knocked Paulo out of the way and sent the untouchable sprawling.

Paulo got up. He had to get that piece of paper

before it disappeared even further in the mire of waste. The untouchable assumed a squatting position, looking at the cow but no longer trying to claim his territory. Paulo plunged his arms back in, dodging the cow's handlebar horns. The animal delved around and shifted its feet. Paulo hopped aside, acutely aware that he was wearing scrappy little sandals. Cows' hooves were very sharp. They could slice into bare toes like a cleaver.

The cow came up for air and Paulo saw it – a strip of paper with red writing, sticking below the cow's left eye. He took hold of one of the horns and steered the head towards him, just as he would if he was trying to move one of the beasts on his parents' ranch.

A man screamed behind him. Paulo thought it was the untouchable. Then he caught a glimpse of a neat jacket with a Nehru collar and the next thing he knew blows were raining down on his shoulders, back, arms and head. His attacker was a dignified-looking man; the weapon an old-fashioned walking stick – which he raised above his head and brought down hard on Paulo's shoulder. The blow was sharp but feeble, more angry than vicious. As it connected, the crowd shouted and the man hit him again. Paulo realized he was being given a beating – for taking hold of the cow.

He could have fought the man off, but that might have caused a riot. The cow shifted irritably, snuffling like a rooting pig, not used to competition. Paulo pulled his toes out of the way just in time. As it turned its face towards him, he grabbed the piece of paper and peeled it off like a plaster.

The cow shook its head. Its dung-sodden tail lashed Paulo as he got out of its way. He was prepared for the beating to continue but now the cow was being allowed to root around unmolested, the crowd lost interest. Paulo was invisible once again.

He opened his hand and shook the slimy contents to the floor. The piece of paper stuck to his fingers. It looked like a wrapper from some sort of remedy. It wasn't much, but it might be useful information. He wiped his hand on his loincloth and smuggled the wrapper into his shorts.

Trilok moved on. Paulo let him get ahead a little.

The kidney man didn't walk particularly fast and Paulo's long legs soon made up the distance. He passed Hex and Li, deep in conversation at a stall selling henna. The stall owner was holding Li's hand and drawing imaginary designs on it with his finger. Paulo smiled inwardly. If they had to stay there any longer she'd be getting a tattoo.

The hospital admissions secretary shook her head and handed Amber back her phone with the picture of Bina. 'We don't have her here.' She tapped a few keys on her computer and turned the screen round to face them. 'This is our patient list; you're welcome to look and see if you recognize her yourself.'

Amber scanned the list. Each entry had a thumbnail photo next to it. 'You take photos of every patient?' she said.

'We make identity cards for every patient, with their height, weight, allergies, age, next of kin. It prevents mistakes. Have a look all you want; the only thing I can't do is let you see actual medical records, but you should be able to tell whether your friend is here.'

There weren't many patients of Bina's age listed. Amber clicked on the photos and enlarged them but none of them were her. She scrolled through some of the others.

Alex pointed to a thumbnail. 'Open that one,' he said. Amber clicked on it.

It was the boy he'd just helped, the one sent by the clinic.

That really made him think. He looked at the admissions secretary, expecting to see that she was watching them closely – or calling security. But she wasn't. Unlike the staff at the clinic, she wasn't worried in case they found something.

'I've heard you're the place to come to for kidney transplants,' said Alex.

'Yes,' said the woman. 'We've got one of the best transplant teams.'

Now the crunch question. 'Do you do transplants from live donors too?'

'Yes, sometimes,' said the woman. 'Sometimes it's the only way because there's such a shortage of donors.'

'So people come here to buy kidneys?' said Amber.

The woman shook her head vehemently. 'Certainly not. It's illegal to sell body parts. The government is trying to stamp it out. Some transplants are from live donors, but they're from family members or close friends only. We won't do any operation that hasn't been approved by a government committee. They check all the paperwork and make sure no money changes hands. The hospitals get surprise visits from inspectors to check the paperwork is correct. That's why we're so open with information. Go ahead. Look all you want.'

Amber flicked through a few more files out of politeness but they'd already seen enough. The hospital wasn't hiding anything. They weren't going to find Bina here.

20
MEN IN POWER

Once out of the market, Trilok moved with more purpose. Paulo felt exposed away from the crowds, where people were deliberately trying not to look at him. He limped a little, to look unhealthy. The buildings were different: the street was dominated by a five-storey building that had been a mansion in the nineteenth century, but was now a row of shops with offices above. Paulo noticed Trilok moved as though he was tired – he had to stop or he'd catch him up. He squatted down and pulled out the wrapper, looking at it more closely. It was an Ayurvedic remedy: Triphala. Its benefits were listed: 'For deep cleansing of the colon; laxative and detoxifying. Supports the genito-urinary system.' That meant kidneys, thought Paulo. Well, if he saw the kinds of things Trilok saw, he'd be careful to keep his kidneys in good shape too.

Trilok walked up the stained concrete steps of an office building and went in. Paulo followed, pushing through the glass doors into a wood-panelled lobby with a desk, like a hotel. There was a shriek from behind the desk and a man stepped out, waving a large book like a telephone directory, his voice high with fury.

Hex and Li had followed Paulo. They saw him being ejected down the stairs. Hex climbed over Paulo without looking at him and went into the building.

The man on reception was just sitting down again, replacing the heavy book carefully on his desk. He was giving instructions to a cleaner in a high, hysterical voice, indicating the floor. Good, thought Hex. That meant he'd be too busy to notice anything else. He slipped past towards the lifts and waited for one to arrive. If he acted as though he had every right to be there, he should be all right.

Beside the lift was a list of organizations in the building, in Hindi and English. Hex speed-read it: there were solicitors, a language school, several software companies – but his eye lingered on the last one on the top floor. The General Medical Ethics Committee. Well, well, well, he thought.

Hex took the lift to the top floor. He stepped out into a dingy corridor, keeping one foot in the lift in case he needed to make a quick getaway. At the end was a set of glass doors and a reception desk. He recognized the large figure silhouetted against the window, talking to a receptionist. A secretary walked past with a stack of files.

Hex thought quickly. Could he follow Trilok in? Not a chance. Everyone was dressed in lightweight suits, office clothes. He was wearing a T-shirt, casual trousers and walking boots. He'd be out on his ear in seconds.

He ducked back into the lift and hit the button for the ground floor. As he sauntered out, he looked intently at his palmtop as though deep in thought after a meeting. Nobody challenged him.

When Hex saw his friends, he wanted to laugh out loud. Li and Paulo were still playing their parts. She was staring at him in horror as though she was a tourist who had just come across this pitiful, revolting creature, and he was squatting on the ground, looking up at her pleadingly with his big brown eyes, his hand outstretched. Hex could smell him from across the street; he was certainly doing a convincing job.

Paulo got up and shuffled away. He had to keep up the pretence in case someone saw them. Now they had a new lead to follow, he had to get out of his costume. He ducked into an alleyway, checked he was alone and stripped down to the T-shirt and shorts under his rags.

When Hex and Li caught up with him, Paulo was rubbing the smears of dirt off his arms, legs and face. The filthy shirt, turban and loincloth were in a heap on the ground.

'That worked very well,' said Li. Several paces away from him, the smell hit her. 'Jeez! Too well.'

Hex got out his palmtop. 'The General Medical Ethics Committee was in that building. I wonder what goes on in there? And how ethical it really is?' In the dark alley, the screen of the palmtop reflected blue on his face as he did a search.

Paulo took off the sandals and put them on top of the bundle of rags. 'Have we got somewhere to put these? We might need them again.'

Li was going to put the rags in a plastic bag but the smell was like a force wall keeping her away. She gave the bag to Paulo. 'You'll have to put them away.' She coughed again. 'I can't touch them.'

Paulo stuffed the vile things into the bag. Still holding it, he grabbed Li around the waist and hugged her close, lips puckered. 'Ah, give us a kiss.'

'Don't you—!' Li squirmed away.

'Aha,' interrupted Hex. '*The General Medical Ethics Committee approves transplants from live donors.*' He swore. 'What's the betting he was going to see them about Bina?'

Their RVP was a café on the ground floor of an office building. A ceiling fan worked overtime to cool the small room, while at one end a man stood enveloped in a cloud of steam as he deep-fried pakoras. The five friends ordered ice-cold cans of cola. The steam from the frying made the room like a sauna, but the hiss meant they could talk without fear of being overheard.

Once they'd pooled their information, Alex summed up: 'What have we found today? She's not in the safe house at the clinic. She's probably not in a hospital – they're so worried about being inspected, the last thing they'd do is keep someone prisoner. But she's being kept somewhere.' He sighed and ran a hand through his hair. 'Where haven't we looked?'

'She must be in a medical establishment,' said Li. 'A doctor's surgery or a clinic, because they have to do the tests.'

'She doesn't have to be there all the time,' said Amber. 'The women in the safe house only spend a couple of hours having tests and the rest of the time they're waiting. They're only in the safe house so that when the results come through they're ready for surgery. She could be kept somewhere else and just brought in for tests as needed.'

'When does the hospital come into it?' said Paulo.

'When she's had the tests and it's time for the operation,' said Alex.

'And she has to have the paperwork,' said Amber. 'They won't let her through the door without it.'

'Which is where the Ethics Committee comes in,' said Hex.

'Maybe St Francis is just a very scrupulous hospital,' said Li. 'Perhaps there are others that aren't.'

'After we visited St Francis, Alex and I went to a few others and they're all just as helpful,' said Amber. 'Anyway, we know St Francis did the transplant with that boy Alex met today. He was a live donor who sold his kidney.'

'So they *are* crooked,' said Paulo.

'No,' said Amber. 'They weren't trying to hide the fact that he'd been there. They must have thought he was legal.'

Li picked up her train of thought. 'He must have had the paperwork from the Ethics Committee. That means the committee's crooked.'

Alex was nodding. 'My dad would say if

something comes down to paperwork and government officials, look for your weak link there. There's always somebody who wants a bit more power, or to make some money. I bet Trilok knows the right people to bribe on that committee so that when he's set up a transplant it goes ahead without a hitch.'

'And by then it will be legal,' said Amber. 'But where does he hide Bina until all that's sorted?'

There was a long pause. Everyone racked their brains.

Alex was the first to speak. He ran his fingers through his hair. 'Come on, guys, think. Trilok must have her. Where is she?' He realized the others were staring at him. 'What?'

'Alex,' said Paulo, 'you look as though you have had a fright.'

'What?' said Alex again. He remembered the stuff in his hair and patted his head. 'Oh God,' he groaned.

Li put her hand on his head. 'Stop, stop, stop. You're making it worse.' She flattened his hair down, then smelled her fingers. 'Mmm. Are you using gel?'

Amber smiled; it was an enormous, man-eating grin. 'It smells like the one you use, Hex.'

Paulo looked at Hex. 'You use gel?'

'Big deal,' said Hex unenthusiastically. 'It's only gel. My hair goes really fluffy otherwise.'

'Well, well,' said Amber. 'You live and learn.'

Outside, the rains were starting again. The sky turned dark and they heard a roar like a waterfall. Within moments the street was a river. People walking through it kicked up a wake with every step they took. The street hawker opposite put up an umbrella to protect his golden stack of chapattis, and continued to look at the passers-by in the hope of making a sale.

Alex asked, 'Where's Trilok been using his mobile?'

'The same few places,' said Hex. 'The clinic, the committee offices. And Bina can't be in either of those places.'

'We seem to be getting nowhere,' said Li. 'We've just found out where she can't be.'

'Well that's still a result,' said Hex.

'But how long have we got?' said Li.

'Mootama said the tests were going to take forty-eight hours,' said Paulo.

Li sighed. 'So we've got until sometime tomorrow before she has the operation.'

'Right,' said Alex. 'There's nothing else we can do this evening. Let's find a hostel and get our heads down, then we can be up bright and early tomorrow morning.'

21
MONSOON

The next morning the rains had stopped but the streets were like rivers. Next to the hostel was a canal. Li, who had volunteered to go out early and shop for breakfast, looked from the murky surface of the water to the flooded road and could see no difference – just a low wall to separate the two, like a lane divider in a swimming pool. When Li stepped into the street, the water closed over her boots and came halfway up her shins. The whole city smelled wet, the odours and sounds magnified by the saturated atmosphere. It was a different world.

A little way up the road, a small crowd had formed. A policeman was loading a wrapped figure into the back of a car. It looked like a body.

Li waded towards it. She felt something touch the back of her leg. The clammy remains of a discarded chapatti were clinging to her skin. She shook it off in disgust, wondering what else she might be treading on in the filthy water.

She reached the crowd. The policeman closed the doors of the van and went to get into the driver's seat.

Li picked her way through the water to get a better look. A middle-aged man standing next to her told her, 'It's a young girl. Found in the canal. Such a shame.'

Li's heart skipped a beat. She asked breathlessly, 'Did you see her?'

The man nodded. 'I saw her before they covered her face. She was so young. Such a shame.' He splashed away.

Li waded back. Never mind breakfast, she had to tell the others. Had someone stolen Bina's kidney and dumped her?

There was only one place to find out.

As they walked up the steps into the police station Alex was relieved to see that a different policeman was on duty. Maybe we'll actually get somewhere this time, he thought.

'We came in yesterday to report a friend of ours as missing,' he began.

'If you will just wait,' said the officer on duty, 'I'll fetch Sergeant Chopra. He deals with missing persons.'

Alex groaned inwardly. That was just what he didn't want to hear.

An untouchable shuffled by, a scrubby broom in his hands, and then Sergeant Chopra came out from a back room.

'Hello,' said Alex. 'Have you had any news of our missing friend?'

Sergeant Chopra looked at him without interest. 'We haven't found her.'

Amber tried a different approach. 'We saw a body pulled out of the canal this morning. We're very worried that it might be her.'

'It's not your friend.'

'Have you identified it?' said Li. 'One of the witnesses said it was a young girl.'

'It was an untouchable. It doesn't need to be identified.' The sergeant mopped his brow with a crisp white handkerchief.

Alex looked at the man's large, blubbery belly and wasn't surprised he was hot with that much insulation. Even his neck was fat.

Sergeant Chopra turned away from them and picked up the phone. The five friends got a good view of his ample rear. His tight khaki trousers had back pockets, and something made an oblong bump in the stretched material. An oblong bump that was dirty at the top.

It was Paulo who realized what it was: banknotes.

The sergeant turned back to face them. 'Someone is coming from the crematorium,' he said.

Li couldn't believe it. 'You're not going to do a post mortem?'

'Post mortems are for VIPs. Not street scum. I will call you if there is any news of your friend.'

They turned to go, but the sergeant had one more

thing to say. 'Be careful. Lots of people go missing in Chennai. It's a big place. They often go missing in the monsoon. It's a dangerous time. You should be careful.' The small eyes glittered in the fat face.

'There's something about him that makes me very angry,' Alex said as they came down the steps and splashed back into the street.

'And very suspicious,' said Hex. 'I hope that isn't how he deals with all missing persons – having them burned.'

'Did you see that roll of money he had in his pocket?' said Paulo. 'Very dodgy.'

The road was busier now. Alongside the taxis, cars and motorbikes, men in soaked loincloths pushed carts to the market.

Hex got out his palmtop. 'Hey, let's stop here. I want to try something.' He flipped up the website that allowed him to track Trilok's mobile.

Amber peered over his shoulder, recognizing the image on the screen. 'What's the kidney man up to now?'

'It's not what he's up to now,' said Hex. 'It's what

he's been up to. This is a list of numbers he's called recently – there are a lot to the same one. And – get this – they were all made since we went and looked for Bina in the safe house.'

'Now that is interesting,' said Paulo.

Hex asked, 'Alex, can you see into the police station from here?'

'Yeah. I can see that fat sergeant.'

'What's he doing?'

'Eating. Now there's a surprise.'

'Well he's got to keep his figure,' said Amber.

Hex took out his mobile, keyed in the number he had identified from the website and pressed CALL.

In the window, the policeman put down his snack, wiped his hands, picked up his phone and answered.

Hex heard Chopra's voice say hello. He cancelled the call, his face shocked.

'*Dios*,' whispered Paulo.

'Come on,' said Alex. 'We can talk while we're walking.'

They plodded through the water until they were well away from the police station. Amber was the first to speak.

'So Trilok calls the policeman a lot. A policeman's a rather unusual friend for a man with an illegal trade.'

'Exactly,' said Hex. 'Why are they such close buddies?'

'Because,' said Alex, 'Chopra's watching Trilok's back and keeping him out of trouble.'

'And,' said Paulo, 'he just got paid this morning – that money in his pocket.'

Hex tucked his palmtop away. 'He certainly didn't get as fat as that on a normal policeman's wage.'

Amber snorted. 'I'd bet my bottom dollar Sergeant Chopra knows where Bina is.'

'We've got to look at that body,' said Alex. 'I just know there's something up about that body.'

'They've got a cleaner who's an untouchable,' said Paulo. 'They won't notice another.'

'Especially if it's someone really small,' said Li.

22
INTO THE MORGUE

The desk was unmanned. Li had her chance to sneak in. The turban was like cardboard, stiff with unmentionable stains. She had wrapped part of it around the lower half of her face and the rough material chafed against her cheek. Every breath she took it touched her lips. The smell made her want to gag. How had Paulo managed to wear this? There was a fresh streak of fruit and vegetable slime on the loincloth where he had wiped his hands after delving into the bin. Flies stuck to it.

She went behind the desk and into the corridor

behind. She passed an office. The walls were covered with notices and photos in varying stages of yellowing age. Two officers sat at desks reading paperwork. They didn't notice her.

There was the sound of a toilet flushing. Sergeant Chopra flung open the bathroom door. He was standing right beside her. Sweat ran down his face and he mopped his brow.

The next second a blow to her head set her ears ringing. Li steeled herself not to respond. Normally she would have had him on the floor in an instant but she had to be appear submissive.

Chopra shouted something at her in rapid Hindi and motioned towards the bathroom, then pushed past her into the office.

Li stood at the open door of the bathroom. A row of white urinals was surrounded by dingy green tiles. A powerful, sharp smell made her throat clench. Even the fetid turban in front of her nose was preferable. Holding it to her face, she trudged into the room.

A pool of vomit lay on the floor. Li took one look and then turned away, her stomach churning.

At least she had gained access. She only had to do this and then she could go where she wanted. She went to find a mop and bucket.

Five minutes after Li went in, a motorbike pulled up in the waterlogged street. Its rider, who wore no helmet, cut the engine, kicked the stand down and got off. He took a blue plastic cool box off the back of the bike and went into the police station.

Alex, Amber, Paulo and Hex, watching from the library opposite, had an excellent view.

'Is that Sergeant Chopra's lunch?' said Alex.

'No,' said Amber. 'Look at what he's wearing – that white shirt and tie. He's not a street hawker. He's a professional.'

'A professional what?' said Paulo.

'A professional who's come to see the fat sergeant,' said Alex. 'Look.'

Sure enough, Sergeant Chopra greeted the man and guided him into the station and out of their view.

'He seems to get better treatment than normal members of the public,' said Alex.

'Could be from the crematorium,' said Hex. 'Chopra made a call to them.'

'I hope Li's all right in there,' said Amber.

It was the most revolting thing Li had ever had to do. She tried not to look at the mess she was clearing up but she'd seen pieces of undigested bhaji. She doubted she'd ever eat another of those.

She didn't try to make a thorough job of it, just threw down some disinfectant and swilled up the worst of it. Afterwards, she decided to keep the bucket and mop with her as part of her disguise.

She checked no one was coming, then slipped out into the corridor. Where was the morgue? To her left was a stairwell. Morgues were more likely to be below ground. Hoisting mop and bucket, she went down.

Sergeant Chopra was coming up. She hid her face, but he pushed past her as though she wasn't there. She caught a glimpse of his ample backside. Was it her imagination, or had the wad of money got bigger? Had Trilok just been there? Or was someone else paying him?

At the bottom of the stairs, she stepped into dark water. The basement had flooded. The cracked tiles were pale, like plants starved of light. In one direction was a barred gate: the cells. Reflected in the black water, the bars looked as though they extended down for ever.

In the other direction was an open door leading to a tiled room. Li caught a powerful zing of disinfectant and something else that it couldn't hide: a sickly, heavy odour of death. That must be the mortuary.

Li waded slowly towards the room, making the water lap against the tiles. She turned round – was she being followed? No, it was just the water, beating like a live thing around her. The river Styx, flowing towards the dead. Her heart was pounding. What would she find in the mortuary?

Four porcelain benches stood in the middle of the room. The three furthest away from her were occupied by still figures under grubby sheets. At least they were covered; Li was thankful for that. The slab nearest to her was empty. Its surface was worn and yellowed with years of bleach, chemicals and blood. Rusty stains showed where excretions from dead bodies had been hosed away.

There was a man in the room, pulling a sheet over one of the bodies. He wore a white shirt and a tie, a green plastic apron, and surgical gloves and mask. It was impossible for Li to move quietly through the water, but he ignored her anyway and fastened the lid on a blue cool box. He took off his apron and mask, peeled off his gloves with a snap, and threw them at her, saying something sharp in Hindi. Then he picked up the cool box and waded to the door. The discarded mask, gloves and apron turned slowly on the surface of the inky water.

Li was alone. She moved towards the body. She could see contours under the sheet – the silhouette of a nose and chin, the rise of a girlish pair of breasts, long legs, feet. It could be Bina. Maybe she could tell without having to lift the sheet. For instance, was this girl the right height?

Next to the head was an odd-looking tool. Li picked it up. It was like a long slender pair of scissors, with a pair of curved paddles instead of blades. It might be evidence. She put it in her pocket. The shrouded body waited. She would have to inspect it. She picked the gloves out of the black water and put them on.

She gripped the corner of the shroud but something stopped her moving it. A thin red substance was trickling around the head, like watery blood. It was like a warning not to look.

Li looked at the sink behind her. There was a crumpled pile of yellow sponges, with wrappers from the gloves. What had been done to the body? That man had obviously cut something out. She envisaged bloodied holes. The strange scissors in her pocket dug cruelly into her hip.

Maybe she could just look at the face and see if it was Bina. She pulled back the sheet.

She moved back immediately and looked away but the image persisted on her retinas. Where the eyes should have been were two empty red hollows.

That man had taken out the eyes.

23
THE COURIER

Li looked anywhere but at the eyeless face. Reflections from the water threw giddy patterns on the walls and ceiling. She would have to look again. The first glimpse had told her it was a female, but she had to know if it was Bina.

Li put her hands over her eyes and lowered her head. She opened her fingers a crack and looked at the face again.

It wasn't Bina.

She quickly pulled the sheet over the face, hiding the horrible disfigurement. She moved further down the body and lifted the sheet again. The dead girl wore a dirty green shift. Her wrists were emaciated, the bones showing clearly, the skin shrunken – probably she died of malnutrition in the slums and ended up in the canal because her family couldn't afford a funeral. Li felt sad for her. What a horrible life. No foul play, anyway – at least not while she was living. Until someone stole her eyes.

Li looked across to the other two bodies. The water shadows lapped over their shrouds but they were like rock. It was hard to believe that something of flesh and blood could be so still.

Li decided she'd better check those too. One of them could still be Bina. She paddled through the murky water to the next one and pulled back the sheet.

The same horror awaited her: the eyes had gone. But this time Li was better prepared. It was a man, quite old and thin – probably one of the many beggars who'd died in the streets. Li covered him quickly. On a hunch she had a quick look at his abdomen in case his kidney had been removed, but the thin body was intact.

She moved onto the third corpse. This one was younger and had a large gash on his head, his hair matted with congealed blood. In amongst the mess of that, the eyes had been carefully removed – taken out neatly, the eyelids left intact, even the eyelashes undisturbed. Not a single cut had been made anywhere else. It was a neat, professional job, surgical and precise.

A professional job. Someone who took out eyes all the time. Was it legal to take them from unidentified bodies in a police station? No, she decided, it probably wasn't. That was probably why Sergeant Chopra's roll of banknotes was looking bigger than before. He had sold these people's eyes.

Li got out her phone and keyed in a text.

Alex got the message just as the man with the cool box was padding down the steps of the police station. By the time he had fixed the box onto the back of his bike and started the engine, Alex was out in the street. A motorized rickshaw was pulling in to the side of the flooded road. With no taxis in sight, Alex flagged it down.

The rickshaw driver got off. Alex splashed up to him. 'How much to hire?'

The driver shook his head. 'Lunch.'

Alex wondered whether it was a negotiating tactic, but he didn't have time to play games. The bike was getting away, weaving between the traffic that churned through the dirty water. Alex got a roll of notes out of his pocket. 'I'll drive it myself. How much?'

The driver took a samosa out of a battered plastic container and took a bite.

'How much to hire?' said Alex again.

The man spoke through a mouthful of samosa. 'Four hundred rupees.' He held up four fingers.

It sounded like a lot, but it was about four pounds. Alex handed over the money. The man gave him the ignition keys, grinning broadly, and tucked the money into his top pocket.

Alex got on, gunned the engine and moved off.

Hex, Amber and Paulo were still in the library, waiting for Li.

'What was the rush?' said Hex.

'I don't know,' said Amber. 'Li just told us to follow that man.'

They watched Alex steering through the traffic, beeping like crazy. The rickshaw was a peculiar vehicle: the front end a single motorbike wheel, the back wheel replaced by two bicycle wheels and a wide seat. The handlebars were great tall things that forced him to sit back as though he was waterskiing.

'I wouldn't have picked that as a pursuit vehicle,' said Paulo. 'It's going to be a nightmare to ride.'

Alex heard honking behind him. He turned and the bonnet of a brown Honda swerved past him, drenching him with filthy water. Alex ducked and one of the back wheels left the ground. He sat up again, wrestling with the huge handlebars. The bike was really unstable. He'd have thought three wheels would have been better than two.

The controls weren't that different from the quad bikes he had driven. But that was on dry land; riding in a virtual lake was very different. Alex tried to get up more speed, but the drag was so strong, it was like trying to move through treacle. He reached forty-five k.p.h. and the front wheel started to wobble like crazy. He began to wonder why the owner had been so willing to hire it out to him. Perhaps he hadn't hired it; he'd sold it.

The motorbike was now crawling, so Alex was able to catch up. A cow stood dozing in the road, and cars, bikes and pedestrians were going every which way like a watery dodgem ride. The courier slipped past and sped away.

Alex revved his engine. The gap between them mustn't widen. The rickshaw merely chugged along. Alex glanced down at the petrol tank as if to remonstrate with it – and did a double-take. There was a Harley Davidson logo. The classic American bike. Even Alex, who wasn't much of a bike junkie, knew he was sitting on a collector's piece. Paulo, a real petrol-head, would be green with envy.

The bike ahead had slowed and Alex tried to close the gap again. He gunned the engine, but it responded sluggishly. If this was a classic machine it was a bit disappointing. He looked at the logo again. It said *Hardley* Davidson. An Indian-made copy.

The bike swerved around a goat. Alex shifted his weight to do the same but nothing happened. The rickshaw steered like a dinosaur. The goat saw doom approaching and hurried out of the way, its eyes rolling.

The motorbike had slowed to get through a narrow gap between two buses. Both were fully loaded with passengers who spilled out of the windows, making the vehicles rock like boats on choppy waters. Alex swerved onto the pavement to pass by. He felt the bump as the wheels mounted the kerb, then an even bigger bump that nearly tipped him over as he came back down. He fought the tall handlebars again and had to slow up. The rickshaw lurched to the side again and stayed there.

Had he got a flat tyre? Alex glanced over his shoulder.

He hadn't run over anything; he'd acquired a passenger. A tall man with the beginnings of a paunch and big white teeth, a Hawaiian shirt and a baseball cap grinned at him. 'Holiday Inn,' he said in an American accent, and settled back. The movement pulled the front wheel off the slippery ground.

Alex sighed. 'I'm not taking passengers,' he called.

Something slapped him on the back. The American had hit him with his baseball cap. 'Holiday Inn, and step on it.'

Steel entered Alex's soul. The blow wasn't hard, but it was intensely rude. He accelerated away. Right, he thought. You're coming with me.

Another flick. 'The Holiday Inn's the other way.'

Alex ignored him. The courier turned his bike into a side street. A taxi was coming and Alex leaned on the horn then swerved in front of it, missing the bonnet by a whisker. One of his back wheels came off the road and the whole bike tilted. His passenger was a big unbalancing lump of ballast.

Flick. The hat came down again. 'Are you some kind of a nut? You nearly had me off.' Flick. 'You! Are you listening?'

Ahead, the road was blocked by a huge train. For a moment Alex goggled at it. Then he realized they were at the station. The tracks were hidden by the water.

'Don't think I'm giving you a tip,' said the voice behind him.

The courier zipped sharply to the left and Alex lumbered after him. The back end of the rickshaw swung violently like a giant, heavy tail. There was a splash, and suddenly the bike felt light again; Alex shot forward. He grappled with the upright handlebars to steady it. When he glanced back, the passenger was on his hands and knees in the water.

Alex grinned. 'Don't worry about the tip,' he called.

Free of his burden, he roared up to the station entrance, a grand building like a gothic cathedral. The courier was dropping off his bike at a hire stall. Then he unclamped the cool box and ran in through the gothic archway.

Alex parked the rickshaw, hid the keys under the seat and splashed after him. Running through the water was easier than driving. When he bounded up the steps onto dry land he felt suddenly free.

The courier was running to one of the platforms. Alex followed him, dodging families who squatted on the concourse with large cloth bundles of belongings. The courier jumped onto a train that was belching grey diesel fumes into the rafters, ready to go. The whistle blew as Alex pounded through the barrier. The train began to move. Alex sprinted, fast. He reached an open door, grabbed the handle and swung in.

Gasping for breath in the space between the compartments, he took out his phone.

24
THE END OF
THE LINE

The bathroom in the hostel was going to be occupied for quite some time. Li was having the longest shower of her life.

Amber, Hex and Paulo sat in the bedroom discussing what she had told them.

'That cool box had eyes in it?' said Amber.

'And Li saw Chopra with another lot of money,' said Paulo. 'So he's selling the eyes of random bodies who turn up at the morgue.'

'Why would anyone sell eyes?' said Amber.

'Why would anyone *buy* eyes?' said Hex. He was already tapping on his keyboard. 'There's only one way to find out— Aha. Transplants. And there's a huge shortage of donor eyes.'

Amber nearly gagged. 'They transplant whole eyes?'

'No,' said Hex. 'Just the cornea: the transparent flesh at the front. It covers the iris and the pupil. If it gets diseased you go blind. A cornea transplant literally opens the curtains again.'

Paulo was also finding the idea hard going. 'But eyes from dead bodies? Bodies that have been in the water all night, or found in the street? Don't donors have to at least be – er – fresh?'

Hex was reading from a website. '*Harvesting an eye* . . . blah blah blah . . . *must be done within six hours of death. It can be done anywhere with simple instruments.*' He looked up. 'So you don't need an operating theatre. Just whip the eye out.'

Amber winced. 'Yes, thank you, Hex, we get the picture.'

Hex noticed her discomfort. 'Get a spoon. *Ping.* Out it comes like a billiard ball.'

'Yes, thank you, Hex,' said Amber, more fiercely.

Hex continued to paraphrase the website. 'They can be stored in special eye banks. When a donor cornea is needed, it is carefully removed from the eye' – he glanced at Amber – 'with something like a potato peeler – and transported to—'

'Stop, stop, stop!!' She buried her face in her hands and shook her head.

Hex grinned at her and prepared to play his trump card, a gruesome picture on the website. But then his phone bleeped with a message. He looked at the screen. 'It's Alex . . . he's on a train.'

'A train?' said Paulo. 'Going where?'

'He doesn't say – must still be following the courier.'

'How's Alex getting lost going to help us find Bina?' asked Amber.

'Think about it,' said Hex. 'It's part of the black market in organs, right? There's Trilok, who sells kidneys, and there's Chopra, who sells eyes. Chopra helps Trilok keep out of trouble. Now suppose Chopra is helping him hide Bina? Where would be a nice, secure, out-of-the-way place? A nice, secure medical establishment. Which is no doubt where the courier is headed.'

Li came in, combing her fingers through her wet hair. She was back in her normal clothes.

'I get it,' said Paulo. 'The eye bank where Chopra makes regular deposits.'

Li sat on the bed. 'But it might be miles away. Bina must be quite close to here because she has to be brought back for the operation.'

Hex texted Alex: 'TRAIN 2 WHERE?'

He got an answer back promptly. 'COLOMBO FORT. STOPPING TRAIN.'

Paulo spread a map on the bed. With his fingers he traced the railway line. 'Chennai to Colombo Fort . . .' He looked at Hex. 'He can't be. Colombo Fort is in Sri Lanka.'

For a moment the room was silent. Alex couldn't be going all the way to Sri Lanka, surely?

Hex had a brainwave. 'Wait a minute. Alex said it's the stopping train. If the bike guy was going all the way to Sri Lanka he'd take an express. After all, he's got to get his eyes in the fridge.' Amber glared at him but he carried on. 'But stopping trains are for people who aren't going very far.'

Amber finished the thought for him. 'He's getting

off at a local station. He's not going very far at all.'

'Exactly,' said Hex. His phone bleeped again. Alex had sent another text: 'TELL DRIVER RICKSHAW AT STN. KEYS WEDGED INSIDE SEAT COVER.'

'Are we better off looking in Chennai or following Alex?' asked Li.

Paulo said, 'I think Alex will need backup. He shouldn't go in there on his own.'

'But we'd better keep an eye on what's going on here too,' said Li.

'Well, I'll have to stay here,' said Hex, 'because I can track Trilok. I can track you guys too.'

'Who else is up for a mystery train ride?' said Paulo.

Li and Amber both leaped to answer: 'Me!'

Paulo looked from one to the other. If he had to choose, who would he take?

But Li could see Amber was bored after sitting around in the library. Unless specific skills were needed, they tried to share out the action equally. 'You go,' she said to Amber. Her mouth twitched. 'Go and see the lovely eyes.'

* * *

It was easy to spot the courier: he had the blue plastic cool box balanced on his knee. Alex found a seat nearby and watched the drowned city slip past, then the peeling suburbs. The train stopped every ten minutes or so. By the second stop, the orderly squares of paddy fields were appearing; how quickly the city vanished. The water vanished too; no longer held on the surface by a layer of tarmac and concrete, it soaked away into the parched earth.

Just a few metres away, the courier sat, his trousers wet to mid shin, looking like an ordinary commuter.

Hex sent updates by text. Each one subtly changed how Alex was thinking about his target:

'COURIER REMOVED EYES FROM MORGUE BODIES.' Under that professional shirt and tie beat the heart of a grave robber.

'FOLLOW 2 EYE BANK + SEARCH FOR B.' I'll follow you all right. I'm not letting you out of my sight. If I find you've got Bina . . .

'P + A ON WAY.' And I've got backup.

At the third stop, the courier got off. Alex waited, just in case the man knew he was being followed.

Then he sprang out as though he'd just woken up and found himself at his stop.

The platform had no roof. A small station building stood at one end and white cows swished their tails on the veranda. The air smelled of warm, wet vegetation and cow dung. Tufts of grass grew around a battered sign saying PERUNGALATTUR HALT.

Alex followed the courier through the station building and out to a corrugated-iron garage. He stayed well back, watching him with one eye while he texted the name of the station to the others. The courier unlocked a padlock on the garage door. He brought out a mud-spattered bicycle, fixed the cool box on the rack behind the seat and set off round the back of the shed.

Where was he going? There didn't seem to be a road, although all around the ground was thick mud, so a road might have been hidden. Alex stepped cautiously towards the shed. Then he spotted a spur of railway track leading off the main track behind it. Tall weeds grew up between the sleepers; obviously it hadn't been used for some years.

Alex texted another message to Paulo and Amber: 'LOOK FOR SHED ON R. FOLLOW DISUSED SPUR.'

He hooked the phone back on his belt and set off on foot. His target was easy to follow; he kept to the spur line which sliced between the rice paddies. The sun was out and the paddies reflected a brilliant blue sky, but it was a lonely, featureless landscape. Only a few scrubby trees and bushes along the side of the track broke up the monotony of the view – they would just about provide cover if he needed it. Alex jogged at first to make sure he didn't get too far behind, but once he was within two hundred metres of the target he slowed to a walk. That was far enough away to duck into the trees if the man looked back, but close enough to keep an eye on him.

The bike disappeared around a bend. What if it turned off while it was out of sight? Alex sprinted along in pursuit, his feet slipping on the muddy ground. But all was well: the track carried on in a straight line. In the distance stood a square building like a grey box. At first it looked tiny, like a shed, but as Alex drew closer he saw it looked like an old depot. An old depot that had been shored up –

patched with new breeze blocks at the top and corrugated iron at the bottom. A window high up in the wall had been bricked up. The tracks ran up to a pair of rusted buffers in front of the building. The end of the line. Alex shuddered.

The target rode his bicycle round the side and disappeared. There must be a gate or an archway.

Alex crouched beside a tree and texted his new position to Paulo and Amber again. That done, he listened. There were no sounds of activity; no one came out to greet the courier. There seemed to be no security guards he had to get past. Most importantly, he wasn't about to come straight out again – and run into Alex.

There was another, smaller building alongside the main one that hadn't been refurbished. The corrugated iron was rusty and the brickwork old and decayed. It looked empty. Alex crept forwards and chanced a look into its dark interior. Just as he thought: bright patches of sky could be seen through holes in the roof. But it made an excellent observation point for the main building.

Alex crept in and hunkered down by a rusted hole

in the corrugated iron wall. It was opposite the entrance. A square archway, big enough to admit a tall vehicle, led into a brick courtyard, where a couple of vans stood in front of a large set of doors. The vans bore a logo and a name: Vikram Medical Supplies. There was also a smaller copy of the logo beside the main front doors. The name seemed familiar. Why?

Then he realized. While he was waiting for Amber at the clinic, he had seen one of those vans making a delivery. That was an interesting connection. Of course, they might deliver to a lot of places, but it was a link nevertheless. And it obviously did more than collect eyes. What else might it collect?

Alex decided he had seen all he could from this observation point. He still hadn't found a way to get in. He needed to look at some of the other faces of the building.

He ran across to the corner of the main building and peered round. A few metres away was an open window, at ground-floor level. Alex slid along the wall, moving quietly. A few metres away he stopped and listened very carefully. No sound came from inside the building. The room was probably empty. Alex decided he could chance it.

He peeked round the window frame. It was a lab – benches with microscopes, piles of papers and other assorted scientific equipment. And, next to the window, a white lab coat hanging on the back of a chair.

It would make an excellent disguise. Alex peered further into the room, looking for movement, shadows. There might be someone bent over one of those benches, working silently. But no one was there. Alex reached in through the window and grasped the coat. He hooked one shoulder off the chair, then the other. The door opened.

He was past the point of no return now. He whipped the coat out of the window and scooted away to the end of the building where no one could see him. Had he been spotted? He'd soon hear. He kept the coat rolled up in a bundle under his arm. But no one triggered any alarms.

He put the coat on, took several deep breaths and then confidently, calmly, walked in through the archway.

25
BACKUP

'No trains to Perungalattur for two hours.' Amber spat out the words. They had raced to the station by taxi, and while Paulo digested the latest updates from Alex, Amber had tried to get tickets. Now she was back – empty-handed and looking murderous.

But instead of being disappointed, Paulo looked delighted.

'What?' said Amber. 'What's good about that?'

Paulo took her arm and led her out of the concourse. Opposite the station a bored-looking man stood next to a row of motorbikes and a rack of helmets.

'They're Royal Enfields,' said Paulo, his eyes glittering. 'They were being made in the Second World War.'

Amber thought she'd seen bikes like that in black and white films. 'Is an old thing like that really going to go anywhere?'

But Paulo had caught the owner's eye. In moments he'd hired a bike and was steering it away from the stall by its handlebars, wearing two helmets on his arm like handbags. The wheels of the bike swished gently through the water.

Amber pulled on her helmet. Close up, the bike looked even less impressive: all scraped paintwork and exposed shock absorbers. The exhaust looked like a rusty water pipe. But Paulo was looking at the machine with undisguised love. 'Couldn't you get a supermarket trolley or something? It might be faster. Or a surfboard,' Amber suggested.

Paulo straddled the bike and started the engine. It spluttered before settling into a regular thrumming. 'Just get on the dream machine, babe.'

'Do you know where you're going?' Amber said as she got on behind him.

'You're navigating.' Paulo handed her a map he'd picked up inside the station. It was almost torn out of her hands as he gunned the engine and they shot off up the road.

Hex wished Li had gone with Paulo instead of Amber. Li had been pacing up and down the hostel room for the past half-hour, an irritated walk that said she'd been cooped up for too long. They all found surveillance hard – everyone preferred to be in on the action. But Li was going for an Oscar. What would Amber have done? She'd have been hopping up and down too, but somehow it would have been different.

'Hasn't he phoned anyone yet?' said Li.

Hex looked at the mobile phone website for the umpteenth time. As soon as Trilok made or received a call they would know where he was. But until he did, they would wait.

Li didn't even wait for Hex to reply. 'Why isn't he phoning people? He's got a lot to do today. He must have evil henchmen out there waiting for his command.' She hunched her shoulders irritably.

Hex shrugged but didn't say anything. It was interesting how the tension got to them in such different ways. Li got hyper. He preferred to retreat into his own world, just be quiet, get on with it and not think about the boredom. But when the call came through, he'd zap into action.

Li paused by the end of her bed. Hex was making it clear that he would rather watch the website on his own. He wasn't the easiest person to talk to, but Li felt she'd never really got through to him. Right now he was behaving like a real geek but she knew there was more to him than that.

She grasped the bedstead and rocked it with her hands. It should take her weight. She squared up to it, put her hands shoulder-width apart and, with a little spring, pulled herself up in a handstand on the rail. And stayed there.

'Ah, that feels better. Action at last.'

Hex looked at her. Thank goodness she'd found something to do. 'You've got to stay up there until Trilok phones someone.'

'No sweat. That's the first joke you've made for half an hour.' Her voice sounded strained with the effort of holding the position.

'I'm not joking. You've got to stay up there.'

'I will, don't worry. You probably wish Amber was here, don't you? Instead of me.' Li was surprised to find herself saying such a thing. But making small talk didn't work with Hex. If she was going to talk about something she had to get her teeth into it. 'You seem like a computer geek but you've got a soft spot for her.'

'Wouldn't *you* rather it was Paulo here?' rejoined Hex.

Crafty beggar, Li thought, watching his face. He hadn't let his expression change by so much as a flicker. 'I asked first.'

'She's even less patient than you are.'

'No, but you do like her, don't you?'

'You know,' said Hex, 'if we find Bina and bring her back, that doesn't solve the problem. She still doesn't have a dowry and neither do her sisters.'

'Don't change the subject. Answer the question.'

Li's voice was sounding even more strained. It really was hard work staying up there.

'I'll answer the question if you stay up there for another' – he looked at his watch – 'minute.'

'Start working out what you're going to say.' Li's wrists were burning, the heels of her hands numb from taking her weight. But she wouldn't give up. Not now.

'In the meantime, what about Bina and her dowry?'

An answer popped into Li's head. 'We finish the school. They get educated and get jobs. Then they don't have to marry and pay big dowries to stay alive. There. The world's problems sorted if you just look at them upside down.'

Hex was amused. 'That question was obviously too easy. What's the square root of zero?'

Li screwed up her face. 'Huh? That's daft. How long before I can come down?'

But Hex was looking at the screen. When he replied, his voice had changed. 'Well, what do you know . . .'

'What's happened?'

Hex was looking at the screen. 'Trilok's mobile provider says it's time to send him a bill.' He read off the screen. '*Check address*,' it says.' He clicked a button. 'Yes please.' Another screen came up. Hex smiled, a slow but very satisfied smile. 'Got you.' He turned the palmtop round so that Li could see it.

Li tried to read the screen, but this destroyed her concentration. She wobbled and fell down. Immediately her hands and arms throbbed.

Hex was excited. 'This is his home address. The one place we haven't searched.'

Li was on to his train of thought straight away. 'Could be where he's got Bina.'

'Or some really important clues. We've got to check it out.'

They raced down the stairs and splashed out into the street. 'Don't think you've got out of answering my question,' Li said to Hex.

'You didn't stay up there long enough,' he grinned.

But for now, they put their minds on the job in hand. 'Taxi?' asked Li. 'Or shall we go on foot?'

26
EYE BANK

Alex padded down the corridor, a stack of papers in his arms. He had picked them up in the reception of Vikram Medical Supplies and hoped they would make him look like he was busy doing something official.

The next room was a lab. A woman sat working at the bench, face shielded by a mask, forearms visible above her gloves. Alex went cautiously in to get a better look at the room, holding up the papers as though he was consulting them. There was a large magnifying glass suspended on a frame above something on a white tile. The something was roughly the size of a ping-pong ball, slightly pinkish. Alex's heart skipped a beat. It was an eye. The pinkish colouring was streaks of blood on the white. The technician peered through the magnifying lens and moved the tip of the scalpel towards the eye, just by the brown iris.

She was removing the cornea. Alex blinked hard in a reflex act of protection.

Without looking up, the technician spoke: 'Have you come to clear the waste?'

If Alex didn't reply, she might look up and see she didn't know him. If he played along, she would probably just concentrate on what she was doing. 'Yes,' he said.

'It's down here,' said the woman, still looking through the magnifying lens. She pointed to a yellow plastic bag on the bench beside her. She cut carefully around the iris of the eye, as though drawing a circle.

Alex went up to the bench; the woman was absorbed in her task. He was horrified but at the same time fascinated by what she was doing. With a dropper nozzle she shook a few drops of saline onto the eye to keep it moist, then laid the scalpel flat against the eyeball.

That was nearly too much for Alex. He saw the blade glide slowly over the brown iris and pupil and nearly threw up. He willed his heaving guts to calm down. Anything he did, any noise he made might betray that he wasn't used to seeing this.

He picked up the yellow bag and moved towards the door. He looked in the bag, then wished he hadn't. It contained several butchered eyeballs. The naked brown irises, shorn of their protective corneas, were drying. Their dull surfaces looked like the gills on the underside of mushrooms. A clear jelly oozed through the black hole of a pupil. From biology lessons Alex knew this was aqueous humour, the fluid in front of the lens. He twisted the neck of the bag tightly shut and blinked hard, squeezing his eyes so that tears lubricated them. But in his mind's eye he could still see those desiccated irises. He'd never eat lychees again.

Still, there was nothing more to see in the lab. He went out into the corridor. The yellow bag of spent eyes gave him another useful prop.

The next door bore a sign saying WAREHOUSE. He opened the door. There were racks of white boxes. As Alex moved along, he saw that they were labelled as bandages and dressings. At the end of the row was a walk-in fridge about the size of a small van.

The door was open. He peeked in cautiously. Inside were more boxes – some of them drugs. There was also what seemed to be a tray of large ice cubes. Ice cubes? Alex looked closer.

The trays didn't contain ice, but chilled colourless liquid surrounding an eyeball, waiting to be processed. This was the eye bank.

There was nothing else to see in the fridge, and Alex was about to go out. Then he heard the outer door of the warehouse shut. Someone was coming in.

There was nowhere to hide except further in the fridge. Alex took down a box of drugs and pulled the door to, propping it open with the box, then crouched in the shadows by the door and listened.

He heard boxes being dragged off shelves and people talking. Two, possibly three. Probably putting together a delivery of those dressings and whatever else was out there. He hoped they wouldn't need anything from the fridge.

They seemed to take for ever. Alex's breath was showing in clouds of condensation. For the first time since he had arrived in India Alex felt cold. At first it was a relief, but then it became a chill that went through to his bones. It was worse that he had to sit still so he could hear what was going on outside. What was the temperature?

He heard the voices recede and breathed a sigh of relief. Now he could open the door and get out. He stood up, waving his arms to try to generate some heat.

One of the voices grew louder again. Someone was coming towards the fridge. He was about to be found. His white coat disguise only worked from a distance. Close up in a small area, he was pretty distinctive with his blond hair and English complexion. Silently, he reached for a crate of drugs. He'd hold it in front of his face so that at least the most obviously alien part of him would be concealed. If necessary he could use it as a weapon.

The box that was propping open the door was

kicked into the fridge. The door slammed. The lights went out. The voices receded.

Alex felt for his phone. His fingers felt sluggish, as if they didn't want to move. He grasped the phone clumsily and looked at the screen.

There was no signal. Of course – the walls must be thick with insulation. He couldn't phone for help or send messages.

He could use the blue light from the screen as a torch – a not very powerful torch. He shone it along the wall and found the door. There must be an internal release switch. He felt all around the door. The metal surface was cold and slippery with condensation. He could hardly bear to touch it; it made him feel even colder. He searched the door up and down. Where was that switch?

There wasn't one.

OK, then he had to break out. He started to search the shelves. Was there anything he could use? He ran the phone light over the cardboard boxes. No; just drugs in there. The frogspawn dots of the eyes were next. Alex shuddered, and not just with the cold.

He had to get out. He could jump up and down to keep warm but he couldn't do that for long. He flashed the makeshift torch around the walls. There must be some way to get out. If he didn't – and soon – he would freeze to death.

27
CLOSING IN

Hex and Li were looking for apartment number five on the second floor of a complex arranged around three sides of a central courtyard. It looked expensive but the white stucco was already peeling. Nothing withstood the monsoon rains.

The two friends strolled along a concrete gallery and straight past number five as though it was not what they were looking for at all. They were checking whether there was any cover; what kind of lock was on the door; whether a window was open; whether anyone was home; whether they would have enough cover to pick the lock.

At the end they stopped and leaned over the parapet, a solid wall that went up to waist height. 'OK,' said Hex. 'Here's what we do. This parapet stops anyone seeing the door from below. I can duck down and have a go at the lock.' He pulled a couple of probes out of the small toolkit he wore strapped to his waist.

'I'll keep watch, then once you're in I'll wait down on that bench.' Li pointed to the gardens. 'In case the others call in.'

'I'll be as quick as I can,' said Hex.

'And Hex? Is your phone off?' She smiled.

Hex knew it was but he double-checked to be sure.

They walked back to number five. Li went on a little further and stood near the stairwell. Hex dropped down to his knees in front of the white door. This had to be fast. He slipped a probe into the lock and felt around. It took him a minute. Could do with being faster, he thought. That's something I'd better practise.

The door swung open. He listened, still sitting

back on his haunches, ready to roll away out of sight. Silence. No one was coming to see why the door was open. Hex went in and pushed it closed.

The flat was small and tidy. He had the feeling as soon as he walked in that no one was home. So much for hoping to find Bina. But now he was here, there might be some clues to pick up.

He went into the living room. There was expensive hi-fi and a large TV with a satellite box. Was there a computer? A computer with records on it would be very handy indeed. There was a rack of CDs, a few books, a lone painting, probably also expensive. On the other side of the room, the dining table and chairs. But no computer.

And no papers, which was more disappointing. Trilok must have paperwork. Where did he keep it?

Hex took in all this while he got used to the noises of the flat. The TV was on standby; it gave off a low hum. Next door he could hear people moving around and voices as they talked. If he knew what was 'normal', he'd know immediately if anything abnormal happened.

Hex moved to the kitchen. There was nothing

worth looking at in there, although the washing-up stacked in the sink would start to smell if it was left for much longer. Back past the living room was the bathroom. It was tiny and basic; no clues there. The bedroom was less neat – the bedclothes were rumpled. Hex opened the wardrobe. People often hid things in wardrobes. No. Just a row of shirts and trousers in pale colours, bearing the labels of local tailors. Hex closed the wardrobe door and went back out into the corridor.

There were no other rooms. He'd searched all he could. How infuriating that there were no records to find. He looked around the living room again. Anything with locked drawers? No. What about the dining table – did it have a cutlery drawer? No. It looked like that was it. He walked back down the hallway to the front door.

Then he heard what he didn't want to hear. Someone had stopped outside the front door and put down a heavy bag. Trilok? If so, why hadn't Li warned him?

Hex's mind worked like lightning. Should he hide in the wardrobe? No; Trilok might come in to change his clothes. He might also go for a shower. Hex looked around. Above him was a loft hatch, where the hallway ceiling had been lowered. He'd have to go up there. What could he open it with?

Leaning in the corner by the front door was a large golf umbrella. Hex grabbed it.

He heard the jangle of keys outside. There was a rasp as one was inserted in the lock. Any minute now the door would be open.

Hex poked the hatch aside with the umbrella. A black hole appeared. He let the umbrella fall, then jumped and pulled himself up into the loft space. He snatched his legs out of the way just as the door opened.

Hex held his breath as a figure came in. It wasn't Trilok. It was a woman in a sari and headscarf. She closed the door and put down a holdall. She unzipped the bag and Hex saw brightly labelled cleaning products and a mop. A maid, who must have already been in the building working in another apartment. No untouchables for the kidney man, Hex noticed.

He realized he was probably going to be up in

the loft for a while, so he might as well make himself comfortable. It was less than a metre high; not an ideal place for someone who suffered from claustrophobia. Very, very slowly, so that he wasn't heard down below, he eased himself into a lying position. That was better. The ceiling wasn't so close to his head.

Using his phone as a torch, Hex saw that there was an old suitcase by the entrance to the loft. It was probably empty, but he thought he might as well have a look. He slipped the catch and opened the case.

Inside was a stack of documents. The top ones were marked: ST THOMAS'S CLINIC, VICTORIA ROAD, CHENNAI.

Hex picked one up and started to read.

Alex sat on the floor of the freezer and reached for the box of drugs he had used to prop the door. He tore off the cardboard packaging and tipped out the contents. He didn't need those. He ripped up the box. His fingers were numb and felt like they didn't belong to him. A sharp stabbing pain in his hand made him stop, breathing hard. A staple in the cardboard had gashed him and it throbbed like crazy.

Alex ran the phone light over it, expecting to see a deep gouge, but it was just a small cut. It must be the cold that was making it hurt so much. He carried on ripping the cardboard, catching himself on another staple because he couldn't feel where it was.

When he had enough pieces, he swept them into a pile with his foot. He took his survival tin off his belt and unwrapped the waterproof tape that sealed the lid. It took him several goes to get his nails under the lid and prise it off. He poked the contents with his finger. For all the feeling he had in it he might as well have poked a sausage in there.

He lifted out a box of matches and managed to slide it open. Grasping the match was like trying to pick a lock wearing boxing gloves. At last he managed to wedge one between his fingers and thumb and scrape it along the box. It flared.

Alex touched the match to the pile of cardboard. Would it catch? The cardboard seemed to be plasticized – probably treated with water-proofing. Great. Instead of catching fire it would give off noxious fumes. He'd die of poisoning before the hypothermia got him.

But then a tongue of flame caught.

Alex lit another corner, just to be sure, then stuffed the matches back in his survival kit. The phone light caught a plume of smoke rising into the air. Alex tracked it up to the ceiling and watched it. Would it work? Was that device in the ceiling what he hoped it was? There seemed to be quite a lot of smoke. Surely it was enough.

Maybe he had got it wrong. A shiver racked his body and he almost dropped the phone.

Suddenly the air was filled with a piercing electronic whistle. Water tumbled from the nozzle in the ceiling, like a shower. Compared with the temperature inside the fridge, it seemed warm.

Then he heard what he was waiting for. A clunk, and the door was released. The light came on.

Alex wasted no time. He pulled the door open. No one was about, but outside the warehouse people were running and shouting. The sack of discarded eyes was where he'd dropped it on the floor of the freezer. He stamped out the little fire and stuffed the burnt cardboard in with the eyes. Without evidence, the alert would look like a false alarm.

He checked again that the coast was clear and slipped out. He had to get out of the warehouse. There were other rooms to search. At the door of the warehouse he paused to listen again, then crept out.

Some members of staff stood at the other end of the corridor, putting on visors, preparing to fight the fire. They didn't notice Alex. He ducked through another door so that they could get past.

He was in a darkened room, probably an office. A set of red blinds were drawn against the sun. Well, at least that meant it was likely to be empty. Perhaps he could even come back to this room and slip out of the window when it was time to leave.

He scanned the room. Filing cabinets stood along one wall. There was a desk – and something else. A human form, lying on its back. Alex froze. A worker having a sleep?

Sleeping on what? His eyes strained to make out the details. On the floor, Alex saw a set of wheels. It was a hospital trolley.

A hospital trolley? In an office? Alex crept closer.

The face was turned away from him, but in the red gloom what he could see was looking more and more familiar. Alex approached the figure.

Her sari had been taken away and she was wearing a white hospital gown. A red blanket covered her, as though she was an accident victim. Her eyes were closed and her features looked younger than her thirteen years. She seemed to be asleep.

Bina.

Alex had found her. So this was where they were keeping her.

Should he wake her? Maybe she was drugged. And if he was going to smuggle her out, he'd have to find her some clothes.

Voices stopped at the door and the handle turned. Alex ducked down out of sight.

28
CONTACT

'Perungalattur Halt,' read Amber on the station sign. She tapped Paulo on the shoulder. He stopped, put his feet down and turned, waiting for instructions. 'I'll text Hex and Li; let them know we're here.' As her thumbs worked she said, 'Should we text Alex?'

Paulo shook his head. 'No. He's in enemy territory. We might expose him.'

'OK. I'm done,' said Amber. 'Let's go.'

Truth be told, Paulo was fed up with the bike. It was a real bone-shaker; its suspension was very elderly and every time they went over a bump – which was often – he could feel the shock rattle up every one of his vertebrae. Not only was the bike uncomfortable, it swerved all the time because the shock absorbers were shot. But he wasn't going to say that to Amber. She'd only say, 'I told you so.'

They found the spur line and Paulo tried to stick to the smooth strip of track bed that ran alongside it. But they kept running over pellets of ballast that had strayed from the rails. Paulo felt every one all the way up to his teeth.

The square building came closer. Once they were a few hundred metres from it, Paulo stopped and cut the engine. 'We'd better hide the bike here and continue on foot,' he said. 'We're a bit conspicuous on this.' Amber got off and he wheeled the bike over to some bushes and put the stand down.

The bike was so spattered with mud that it blended in with the landscape quite well. No one would be able to see it unless they came up close and looked.

As they walked, Amber stretched her aching limbs. 'That rust bucket has crippled me.'

Paulo had been moving stiffly but tried to look as though he was perfectly all right. 'It's a classic machine,' he protested.

'It might be in your country; here it's a rust bucket. And you're moving like a knackered old nag so stop pretending you're not.'

As they got closer, they were able to see the layout of the building.

'There's the derelict shed Alex mentioned in his last text,' said Paulo.

'So what's the plan?' said Amber. 'Wait to see if Alex needs us?'

This was always difficult to judge. Go in too early and you could blow someone's cover. Go in too late and . . . it was too late.

'If he hasn't checked in by the next deadline in half an hour,' said Paulo, 'we go in and try to find him.'

They came to the end of the line, where the tracks stopped by the rusted buffers. Despite the heat, Amber felt a chill. There was something desolate about the place. They slipped into the shed from the back and positioned themselves so they had a good view of the courtyard.

People were moving about. A van stood outside the entrance, its back doors open. A man came out of the building, pushing a stretcher on a trolley.

Amber said softly, 'A stretcher? This place doesn't have patients, does it? Alex said it delivered medical supplies.'

The man pushing the stretcher turned it towards the back of the van. He looked up into the rear space, realized he couldn't lift it on his own and called to someone to help him.

At that moment, Paulo and Amber were able to see who was on the stretcher. It was Bina.

'I think,' whispered Paulo, 'they've been delivering other kinds of supplies.'

Amber squeezed his hand tightly. 'We've got to go in. Alex won't be able to get her out by himself.'

Paulo nodded. 'We'd better go now, while they're messing about trying to get her in the back. We'll go for the front and get in the driver's seat. Ready?'

Amber nodded. Keeping low, they came out of the shed and sprinted the short distance to the wall. They stopped and checked. The man at the end of the trolley was discussing with a couple of colleagues how to get it into the van. They all looked occupied.

'Now,' said Paulo.

Still keeping low, they ran for the cab. It was going to work. Paulo had his fingers on the handle.

Suddenly, behind him, he heard a strangled sound. 'Paulo.' He whirled round.

He saw two faces: Amber's frightened, her throat pinned by a strong brown arm. The other face was the face of the courier who had taken the eyes from the bodies in the police station. He was holding a gun to Amber's temple.

'Stay where you are,' said the man in a harsh voice.

Another two staff members came up behind Paulo. He had to let them take his arms.

'I'm sorry,' said Amber.

Paulo could see the frustration in her face.

Amber felt the metal gun barrel prod her temple. She felt the courier's other hand pat her pockets, searching them. She had to stay still and let him do what he wanted; she had no choice.

'What have you got here?' He found the belt

pouch with her insulin and pulled the zip across. The contents spilled out onto the concrete fore-court: the foil-wrapped antiseptic wipes, the brightly coloured insulin injector pens, the spare needles in their protective covering.

'We seem to have a couple of backpackers looking for drugs.' The courier patted the pockets at the front of her trousers, then put his hands in. 'What have you stolen from us, junkie?'

Paulo saw Amber's eyes narrow as the courier explored her pockets roughly. He willed her not to say anything. It was better if they thought they'd come for drugs than if they had to puzzle out why they were really there.

One of the men holding Paulo began to search him. 'I bet they set off the fire alarm earlier too,' he said. He found Paulo's toolkit and hit Paulo with it. 'Is this for breaking and entering?'

Paulo said nothing.

One of the other men was sifting through Amber's spilled possessions. 'These look like insulin pens, boss.'

The courier wasn't impressed. 'Junkies will use

anything that's got a needle. They're crafty as hell.'

Out of the corner of his eye, Paulo saw they had finished loading Bina. A driver was climbing into the front cab. She was going, slipping out of their grasp.

What nobody saw was the blond-haired figure in the white coat and fire mask slip up to the crowd around the van doors. Just as they were about to close them, he strode confidently up and climbed in.

The van did a three-point turn and left the compound.

29
EVIDENCE

Li saw the cleaner leave the flat. Shortly afterwards, Hex came across the grass with a large dusty suitcase.

'What have you got in there? Don't tell me you stole some clothes so you can dress as him?'

'This,' said Hex, 'is dynamite. You've no idea what he's been up to. Let's get back to the hostel.'

Once in their room, Hex bolted the door.

'That bad, huh?' said Li. She opened the case. It contained papers, carefully sorted into folders, with some rather interesting names on them – St

Thomas's Clinic, the General Medical Ethics Committee. 'Dynamite,' she said, nodding.

Hex unloaded some of the papers onto the bed. 'They go back years. It's all the stuff that shows what he's been up to. Look.' He handed her a blue folder. 'Remember the General Medical Ethics Committee, which has to approve live transplants? These papers show payments made to various members. When Trilok has got a transplant match he bribes a couple of people on the committee so they persuade the others to approve it.'

Li was nodding. 'Because if they don't pass it, the sale falls through and he doesn't get his money. But why has he kept records?'

'Because there are several people involved. Any of them could turn nasty, decide to blackmail him. So this suitcase is insurance. If he ever gets arrested, these documents show who accepted bribes and was working with him. That's why he hid it in his loft.' He handed her another stack of papers. 'Look at these.'

Li read the top sheet. 'These are payments made to Sergeant Chopra.'

Hex nodded. 'It's proof that he bribes Chopra to keep trouble away from him. That's why he stalled us every time we went to him asking about Bina. Then he'd tip Trilok off so he could keep her out of our way. But that's not as interesting as' – he took the file from her and swapped it for another – 'this.'

Li read the letterhead. 'They're from the clinic. Test reports.'

'Tissue matching reports. For matching kidney donors. But do you notice something?'

Li looked through the next few pages. 'There seem to be an awful lot.' Some of them had patients' names on them. The same patients' names. 'There seem to be a lot for just a few patients.'

'And,' said Hex, 'look at the handwriting. Compare it with the handwriting on the bribery lists.'

'It's the same.' Li looked up, puzzled. 'Trilok wrote out these reports? He's not a doctor.'

'I think he's forging those reports.'

'Why would he do that?'

'Because he can charge money for them.

Remember the man Amber met in the clinic? He needed dialysis two days a week but could only afford one because he was paying for tests. The doctors said it was a waste of time because he was too ill for a transplant – it would kill him. But Trilok told him he would find a kidney for him and kept finding donors to test. But no matter how many he tested, none were a match.'

Li was immediately on his wavelength. 'Trilok was making that poor man pay for tests – but there was no one to test. That's why the test reports are in his handwriting. He pretends he's having donors tested and pockets the money. That's disgusting.'

Hex looked grim. 'That's not the only patient he's ripped off. There are loads in there, going back years. They stop after a while—'

'Probably because the patient dies.'

'Exactly.'

'He must have bankrupted so many people. Really sick people.' She shuddered. 'Then why does he bother with all that committee stuff? He must make enough money by doing this.'

Hex looked at her gravely. 'Have you ever known

a greedy person who didn't want more money? Besides, it's good for his reputation to have a few successes. His customers die after a while so he has to get new ones. So a successful transplant is a good advert for his business.'

Li shuffled through a few more papers. 'Is there anything in here about the eye bank?'

'I didn't see anything. But I haven't looked through all the papers yet.'

Li riffled through another file. 'Here's some corre-spondence from the Ethics Committee. It's on their headed paper. It's a list of appointments, times and dates, and case histories. One of them's for today.' She handed the paper to Hex. 'Look at this: *Patient seeking second live transplant* . . . Mootama's kidney was for someone who needed a second live transplant . . .'

They realized at the same time. The donor must be Bina.

'When's the meeting?'

Li scanned the page. 'Three-thirty.'

Hex looked at his watch. 'That's in half an hour.'

Li got to her feet. 'Let's take some of these papers;

we'll hide the rest here. If we tell the meeting that Bina was forcibly abducted, we might be able to stop it. Have you got the key to our locker?'

They put the rest of the documents in the steel locker that contained their luggage. When they'd first taken the room two days earlier, Paulo had re-inforced the lock and hinges so it couldn't be forced open. Now they were thankful they had somewhere secure to store the evidence. Then they grabbed the papers they needed, wrapped them in a plastic bag and secured them in Hex's small rucksack. There was no time to lose.

30
TIME RUNNING OUT

Alex crouched behind a delivery crate inside the van. The vehicle gathered speed, the tyres singing out on the wet road surface. That was good. It would help cover any sounds he made. He stood up. Bina was lying peacefully on the trolley, her eyes closed. Was she drugged, or was she trying to stay asleep because that was less frightening than being awake? He'd heard that animals in captivity tended to sleep more than was usual to cope with being held prisoner.

He'd have to try and wake her. But if he scared

her and she cried out, the driver might hear. Gently he put his hand across her mouth.

That was enough. Bina's eyes flew open. Panic dilated her pupils, making her eyes look enormous.

Alex put his other hand up to his lips, indicating that she should make no noise. He kept his voice low. 'It's me, Alex. Remember?'

Under his hand he felt her relax. He took it away. 'We must be very quiet,' he said. 'Are you all right?'

Bina nodded. She tried to speak and it took a couple of goes for her voice to work. She probably hadn't spoken to anyone since she left the village.

'H-have you come to take me home?'

Alex nodded. 'Yes.' Although he hadn't quite worked out how he would do it. Here they were, in a van heading who knew where, the two of them helpless passengers. Bina, though, needed to believe in him. He couldn't let his uncertainty show.

A tear slipped down Bina's cheek. She squeezed her eyes shut for a few moments, as if not wanting him to see. She was talking to herself very quietly. It sounded like Hindi – a prayer of thanks. Alex put his hand on hers, reassuring her. *I won't let you down, Bina. We will get you home*, he told himself.

After a few minutes, Bina had recovered. She sat up and wiped her hand over her eyes.

'Better?' said Alex.

She nodded.

He sat down next to her. 'Do you realize how long we've been looking for you?'

She looked a bit embarrassed. 'Sorry.'

'No need to be sorry.'

'No, it's my fault. I went to meet him. I thought I would help. Mum couldn't get our dowries so I thought I would. I went to meet the kidney man, but he wanted me to come immediately. He was so frightening. I changed my mind. That's when he grabbed me. He put me in a car and took me to Chennai. There was this clinic – the clinic that Mum went to. They took some blood to do tests and locked me in a room. I was so frightened. It was dark and there was this horrible medical smell. I was in there all night. In the morning they gave me an injection and put me on a trolley. I couldn't move. They took me to a van with a load of boxes. Then

I went to sleep. I kept waking up but it was like a nightmare where I couldn't move. Sometimes I'd be in the van; later I was in a red room.'

Her whispering voice made the story even more terrifying. But Alex had to focus on the facts. It all added up. After they had gone looking for Bina at the clinic and reported her missing, Trilok must have whisked her away to the eye bank.

'They drugged me last night and put me in the van again. They drove me back to the clinic in Chennai. I was so frightened. I thought this was it; they were going to do the operation. But they didn't. They did more tests, then drove me back to the red room.'

Alex nodded. So they had done her tests at night. That way no one would ask why she was so drugged, or being ferried in with the medical supplies. He grimaced. How appropriate. Bina was one very important medical supply.

'Do you know if you're a match for the patient?'

Bina nodded. 'Yes. The kidney man told me. I'm a very good match. Just like Mum.' A tear squeezed out of her eye. 'But I don't want to do it. They keep coming and giving me more injections. They are really painful.' She put her hand out and gripped Alex's arm. 'You've got to get me out.'

Her voice was rising. Alex had to keep her quiet. The road noise might provide cover but only while the van was moving fast. If it slowed or stopped unexpectedly, the driver might hear them talking. Alex held her hand and looked at her intently. 'Bina, listen to me. Are you all right? Have you had food, water?'

Bina nodded. 'When they came to give me drugs they gave me a drink of water.' Her whisper was barely audible. 'I didn't want to drink it but they said they'd pump it into me if I refused. They said they had to keep my kidneys working. Every few hours they'd bring me a bed pan and when I'd finished they'd take it away to do tests on it. It was horrible, degrading. I thought they might let me go if there was something wrong with it so I found some red ink in that red room. They said if I did anything like that again they would put a tube inside me take it from me by force.'

Alex winced. The poor girl had been treated like a piece of meat.

'You know where we're going now?' added Bina. 'To the hospital.'

Hex and Li were running through the streets to Mount Road, and suddenly everyone around them was running too. Shoppers at the market stalls were scurrying for cover, trying to protect their heads with plastic bags, boxes – anything that came to hand. Stallholders scrambled to cover their goods. The rain came down, roaring like thunder, and within seconds the shoppers and stalls were shadows in a blurry mist.

Hex shielded his eyes as he ran after Li. He could no longer see her clearly; he had to identify her by the way she moved.

They dashed up the steps of the office building Hex had followed Trilok to. Hex was about to pull open the glass doors, but Li pulled him back.

She steered him out of view. 'Chopra's in there. He must be waiting in case there's trouble.'

'Are you sure?'

Li looked at Hex earnestly. 'Believe me, I'd know him anywhere.'

The doors to the offices opened and a bulky figure

stepped out. Sergeant Chopra. With him were several other officers.

Li hadn't stopped Hex in time; they had been spotted.

'Run!' said Hex.

Li raced after him. 'We don't know those other officers are in on the scam,' she said.

'I don't suppose they are,' Hex called back over his shoulder. 'But do you think they're going to take our word over Chopra's?'

Fat raindrops splashed into their faces. It was like running blind. The rain pelted down and they could no longer see where they were putting their feet. In seconds they were up to their ankles. The street was filling up like a river.

Hex heard Li yell, 'Look out!' and then she grabbed him. A rickshaw was skidding towards them, the driver wrestling helplessly with the front wheel. It slid past him, hit the invisible kerb and capsized.

Li seemed to know where they were going. She ducked into a side street and then up an alleyway. Hex followed. They were running hard, but the policemen were still behind them. The water slowed everything, made their feet slip, their clothes cling to them.

They could outrun the policemen, no problem. But that wouldn't be enough. Time was ticking away. Soon the committee would approve Bina's operation. Once that happened, she was doomed.

Hex grabbed Li and stopped her. 'Bina's case is up in five minutes. I've got an idea. Can you set up a distraction?'

Four khaki shadows appeared at the end of the alleyway. The policemen. 'No problem,' said Li. She looked at the buildings around her. 'Let's go in here.'

It was a building site: a frame of bare concrete walls rising out of the street like a stack of shoeboxes. Scaffolding scaled the outside; spindly tower cranes leaned over the top, rocking in the rain. Li ran in and looked around. Work had stopped because of the downpour.

'This'll do. You do your thing. I'll give our friends a workout.'

Hex scanned the area. He needed somewhere dry. There was a large orange tarpaulin over on the other side of the ground floor. He dashed over to it.

Li stood in the open side of the building site, waiting for the policemen to come past. Their shapes loomed out of the drizzly air like elephants through a mirage. She moved deliberately and obviously and they responded with shouts. They had seen her.

It was show time.

Li sauntered into the interior of the building. She heard heavy footsteps and more shouts behind her and took off at a gentle run. Let them catch up a bit. She had something in mind.

As the policemen started off in pursuit, Li accelerated into her run-up, preparing for her next move.

Above her was a hole in the ceiling; obviously where the stairs would go. Li bent her knees and leaped upwards. Her hands met the concrete lip of the next floor and the momentum plus the strength in her arms pulled her up through the gap. She twisted round into a crouching position and stayed still for a moment, getting her breath – and watching. Down below, the policemen were looking around, shouting angrily.

She stood up. Just as she had thought, there was

another stair-hole further over. She ran over to it at an easy jog and peeped up through the hole. On the ground floor the policemen were getting a ladder so that they could climb up after her.

She looked around. There must be some useful props up here too. Sure enough, a pulley from one of the cranes was dangling through another stair-well from the floor above. Li grinned, an idea forming in her head. She grasped the rope, shinned up it like a monkey and landed lightly on the next floor up.

Then she pattered across to the other empty stair-hole. The police were now two floors below. Sergeant Chopra was holding the ladder and yelling at one of his subordinates to climb up. Li sat down cross-legged and called out to them, waving cheerfully.

All hell broke loose when they saw her. How had she managed to get all the way up there without being seen? Sergeant Chopra shouted at his men. 'Get up there, get after her.'

Meanwhile, Hex scrambled under the tarpaulin and felt around with his hands. Good, it was dry. He got out his palmtop. There wasn't a minute to lose. As if that wasn't enough, they hadn't had a call in from Alex, Amber or Paulo for a while. He had a very bad feeling about it.

'Get in. Now.' As the first van disappeared round the corner, the second van was preparing to set off with a delivery. Amber and Paulo stood impassively, still at gunpoint. They were in no doubt that if they so much as thought about trying to get away or overpowering the courier, he would shoot. They had been in enough troublespots to know when someone was just waving a weapon around and when he would really use it.

Now the courier was telling them to get in the van. The two friends complied. It was something their training had taught them: if you can't see a way out, do as you're told. Look around for escape routes – weaknesses the enemy hasn't spotted – but don't make a break for it unless you're really sure it will work.

'Sit down.'

There was a hospital trolley in the van, along with the boxes. Amber was trying to remain cool but she couldn't help giving Paulo a nervous look. Did the trolley mean they would have their organs stolen, like Bina? The courier had made several phone calls while the van was being loaded, all the time keeping an eye on them. Had he been arranging something with his body-snatcher friends?

Paulo wondered why didn't they just shoot them and take their organs right now? He thought he'd hit on a ray of hope, but then he remembered some of the information Hex had got: organs lasted longer if the donor was alive when they gave them.

Amber and Paulo sat down obediently.

The courier beckoned one of the other staff into the van, then climbed onto the footplate, shadowing him with his gun.

The man tore the wrapper off a pre-packaged syringe and leaned over Amber. A drop of clear fluid bled from its needle and glinted in the sunlight like fresh dew. 'Hold still,' he said.

Amber shrank away. 'What's that?'

It was the courier who answered. 'You'll like this, druggie. See how well we're treating you. This one's on the house.'

Amber stiffened as the needle came towards her. The courier jerked the gun at her. 'Just be a good girl and take your medicine, or we'll tie you down.'

Paulo looked down at the trolley. His left hand was on a webbing strap, about where the wrist would be if he was lying down. There were more restraints on the other side and at the feet. *Dios*, these people were well equipped. He put his hand on Amber's leg, trying to reassure her. He felt her muscles go rigid as she fought her instinct to resist.

She watched as the slender needle sank into her skin, gritting her teeth as the cold liquid flowed into her vein. It hurt; no injection she'd ever had had hurt like this. What were they giving her? If she fought she would get shot. Might that be better? She clenched her teeth together so hard her jaw hurt.

Paulo would be next. The man was ripping open another package for his shot. He held the needle upright like Excalibur. Paulo's mind was racing. What could he do? Amber had had to submit; she hadn't seen any way out. He felt the restraint under his left hand. A desperate plan began to form in his mind.

Paulo held out his left arm. 'This is the arm I prefer,' he said. Might as well play the drug addict.

The courier smiled. 'That's right. No use pretending. We know what you are.'

Paulo smiled back. There was another reason why he wanted them to use that arm. He forced himself to watch the needle slide in as though he was enjoying it. But he could feel the sweat breaking out on his back. What were they giving him? It seemed to take an eternity for the needle to empty. How much were they giving him? He looked at Amber. She was staring ahead; still alert, but inscrutable, unreadable. She wasn't going to give their captors the pleasure of a response. But what would the drug do to her?

Amber was fighting to keep control of herself. Her adrenaline levels were rocketing; there was an alien substance in her system, spreading through her bloodstream, flooding her cells. She was always so careful about what she put into her body; even food was chosen carefully so that she could stay as healthy as possible. Now someone had polluted her body with a drug.

The courier and the man with the needles were leaving the van now. 'We've got to go now,' said the courier. 'Sweet dreams.'

They stepped out and slammed the doors. The sound made Amber come to with a jerk. The drug was taking over. She tried to shake herself awake, but she felt like she was slipping into a warm bath. So, they had been given a sedative.

She wanted to lean on something. She lolled backwards, her head touching the cold metal side of the van. It wasn't comfortable, but it was easier to rest her head there than to sit up. Beside her, Paulo was making a jerking motion with his arm. 'Keep still, Paulo,' she murmured and flicked him with her hand.

Paulo was working fast. As soon as their captors left the van he unbuckled the restraining strap and yanked it off the trolley. He slipped his left hand through up to his elbow and pulled the strap tight. The needle had gone in his forearm, so if he could improvise a tourniquet, he could slow down the rate at which it went into his bloodstream.

They could hear the distinctive voice of the courier in the front of the van,. He was talking on the phone. 'Hello, Sergeant Chopra? The girl is on her way. All tested and sorted. Tell Trilok he owes me one. And you can also tell him if he wants to do it again I've got a couple more donors.'

Paulo had the tourniquet as tight as it would go. His fingers were tingling and going numb; the blood supply was being cut off. He'd have to be careful not to keep it that tight for too long or his fingers would start to die. He only had a short amount of time, then he'd have to loosen the tourniquet and let the drug through.

Amber was lolling back against the side of the van, barely conscious, watching him. With one arm still bound by the tourniquet, Paulo heaved himself off the bench and knelt in front of a refrigerated cabinet. Inside was a row of what looked like ice-cube trays, labelled: CORNEAS READY FOR TRANS-PLANT – KEEP COOL. He swept them aside irritably with his hand. He didn't know what he was looking for but there must be something in there they could use. Before it was too late.

31
THREE-THIRTY

Trilok padded into the back of the room. The General Medical Ethics Committee was in session. The six members sat around a semicircular desk. It was equipped with the latest boardroom technology: there was a general display screen for big presentations and each member had their own personal screen for when they needed to call up extra information.

The meeting was chaired by an elderly man with white hair and a long ivory-coloured shirt. 'Good afternoon, gentlemen,' he said, looking around at the assembled members. 'We're here this afternoon

to review the case of' – he consulted his notes –
'Mr Roy Gopal.'

Gopal. An image sprang to Trilok's head: the
shrunken figure in the bed; the demanding voice on
the other end of the phone, day and night. He'd
started getting migraines whenever the man rang.
No client had been such a tough case. And Trilok
had never had to go to so much trouble to find a
donor. But now the tests were complete and he was
in front of the committee at last. Which was as good
as being home and dry.

Trilok felt like he needed a rest. Maybe after this
he would just concentrate on patients who were no
trouble; the really sick ones who would never survive
a transplant anyway. They just paid their money,
accepted the test results he'd forged and that was
that. They died within a few months, but they died
with hope in their hearts. Certainly it was a much
easier way to make a living than to actually have to
arrange a transplant for real.

The committee chairman was going through the
facts of the case. 'Mr Gopal is about to have his
second transplant. As you know, gentlemen, this

makes it harder to find a match. However, he has a cousin who lives out in the village of Nayla. This cousin . . .'

Trilok nodded to himself as the chairman read out the details. Trilok had written them himself, and handed them over just half an hour before the meeting started. Plus a handful of banknotes. Bina was supposed to be Gopal's cousin. Of course, in real life, there was no way rich old Gopal would be related to Bina's impoverished family in Nayla. The very thought was ridiculous. But so long as the chairman persuaded the others to pass it, the paperwork would be signed and they could whisk Bina and Gopal to the transplant unit.

'There are more details on your screens, gentlemen,' said the chairman, and turned to look at his monitor. Again Trilok smiled to himself. Two other members were also definitely on his side, thanks to his regular payments. That meant three people in all would be arguing for the case, and that should easily persuade the remaining three. For the transplant to go ahead, the committee had to be unanimous.

All the members turned to look at the details on their screens. Then something unexpected happened: Trilok saw an expression he didn't want to see. The three people he thought he could rely on looked worried. Very worried.

Then he heard something he definitely didn't want to hear. The chairman said in a quiet voice: 'I don't think we can approve this one.'

For a moment the room was silent. Then, one by one, the others agreed.

Trilok was aghast. The members he thought he could rely on were rejecting one of his transplants. And not just any transplant; *this* transplant. He could feel his migraine coming on again. He stood up; usually he stayed sitting quietly at the back of the room, but he was so shocked he stood up.

The chairman was looking for him anyway. He beckoned him over, then went back to staring at his screen.

Trilok went and looked at it – and saw something that shouldn't have been there. Trilok knew very well what it was: the details of a Swiss bank account.

'As I said,' the chairman repeated, 'I don't think we can approve this one.' He wouldn't look Trilok in the eye.

The other two members who were in Trilok's pay were looking at him with a similar expression. Shocked; betrayed. He went round to their screens. Each of them showed a message: 'These accounts will be emptied unless the prisoners and the girl are released immediately.'

One of the other members turned to look at Trilok. 'Trilok,' he said quietly, 'who have you been messing with?'

His neighbour had something to say too. He pulled Trilok down by his lapel and hissed into his ear, 'Trilok, if I lose my money, I'm dragging you down with me.'

Trilok swallowed. He straightened up. 'I'll sort it out. Leave it to me.' He walked stiffly from the room.

His migraine was pounding in his head. What the hell was going on? How had anyone found out he was paying committee members? How had they found out the bank account details, for heaven's sake? And what was this about prisoners? What prisoners?

He went down the corridor, past the reception area, out into the lift area and made a phone call.

It was answered immediately. 'Chopra,' he hissed, 'I've got the committee on the verge of mutiny. Has something been going on?'

Sergeant Chopra sounded breathless, like he'd been running. 'Only those kids. But it's all fine now.'

'What kids? Who are these kids?'

'The kids who came to the station looking for the girl. Remember I phoned the clinic and told them to move her?'

'You said that was sorted.'

'I thought it was. But they kept sniffing around. They even managed to tail her to the Vikram depot. So—'

Suddenly it all made sense to Trilok. 'You took them prisoner?' He couldn't believe it. 'You took some kids prisoner?'

Sergeant Chopra sounded irritated. 'That's what you pay me for, isn't it? You don't know what I have to do sometimes to watch your back. And you can hardly get all high and mighty about kidnapping.'

'That was different. She asked to meet me, then got cold feet. Once she's done it she'll be glad she has. But you've taken some kids prisoner?' Trilok repeated it again, disbelieving. 'Chopra, you've gone too far. I never wanted you to do anything like this!'

'What's the matter, Trilok? Losing your nerve? I've got a couple of donors on the way. Kidneys, eyes, hearts, lungs – anything you like. Maybe that will change your mind.'

Hex was still under an orange tarpaulin on the building site. The villains were putty in his hands, all held captive by their greed – and by what he was managing to do with one small but very powerful palmtop. He had hacked into the computer system at the General Medical Ethics Committee and organized that little display with information from Trilok's documents. He had timed the information to appear five minutes after the meeting started – just long enough for everyone to settle in, say hello and get comfortable. Then he sat back to imagine the chaos.

He heard a familiar voice near him and peeped out from under the tarpaulin. Standing no more than a few metres away was Sergeant Chopra. He was on the phone, having an argument. Hex heard a word that chilled him: 'prisoners'. When he had sent the e-mail mentioning prisoners he had only been guessing, given that he hadn't heard from the others in way too long – but here it was confirmed. Amber, Paulo and Alex were prisoners.

Hex withdrew hurriedly, like a turtle into his shell. He whipped out his phone. As well as being able to snap photos it could also take short amounts of video footage. He activated it and peeked out from the tarpaulin, videoing the policeman as he argued with Trilok. While he was doing that, he put his palmtop carefully away. It had done its job.

Sergeant Chopra finished his call. Absorbed in videoing, Hex failed to notice another figure approaching. It was only when a boot nudged his hand that he looked up – into the barrel of a police gun.

32
PASSENGERS

Alex had his ear to the partition between the back of the van and the driver's cab. It was mounted on a slide, like the screen in a taxi cab. It would probably be noisy to move slowly. If he was going to make a move it would have to be short, sharp and sudden. But when?

It sounded like there was only one person in the front; he hadn't heard any conversation throughout the whole time they'd been travelling. The road noise had got louder and more liquid as the rains came again. They hammered on the roof like nails on a tin can. Now and again Alex did hear a noise from the front: the driver was swearing as he negotiated some obstacle in the rain.

The van was stopping more frequently. Alex guessed they must be hitting traffic lights and junctions, so they must be nearly in the city. That was good because the driver would be more preoccupied with traffic.

The pelting of the rain suddenly became ferocious, like chains being dragged over the roof. If Alex was going to make a move, it had to be now, while the noise inside the van would block out any sound he made.

He slid back the partition. The driver was hunched forwards, peering out from under his baseball cap through the windscreen at the rear lights of the vehicles in front. The wipers were on top speed but still they couldn't clear a path through the blurring water.

Alex launched himself through the partition, pulled the cap down over the driver's eyes and yanked on the handbrake. The van jerked, then skidded on the wet road. The driver looked round, but Alex was leaning over him and had the door open. The driver gave a yell and tried to grab his attacker, but Alex knew exactly what he was doing. He grasped the man's belt and shirt, and tipped him out of the open door.

Alex pulled the door shut and locked it, settling in the driver's seat. In his wing mirror he saw the driver get up, confused by the cars that tooted around him. In the rain everything looked as though it was melting. Two cars ahead Alex could just make out a police car. If the driver started trying to catch up, they might come and investigate. The last thing Alex wanted was to attract the attention of Sergeant Chopra and friends. The traffic lights changed. Thank goodness. Alex floored the accelerator.

The van jerked to a halt, the dashboard lights blazing. He'd stalled. Cars beeped ferociously and cut around him from behind. He started the engine again, trying to keep calm. This was nothing like a motorbike or a quad, where you did everything with your hands. There were all these pedals. What were they? Clutch on the left, brake in the middle, accelerator on the right. Keep foot on clutch all the time, that's what Paulo had said.

In the mirror Alex saw the driver running towards him. He put both feet down, clutch and accelerator. The engine rattled. Was it going to stall again? But then the gear bit and he moved off slowly – too slowly. The other traffic was overtaking, beeping irritably. He needed to change up a gear. Left foot down, hold speed with right foot, pull back on gear lever. The engine screamed, then got into the next gear with a great clunk. Alex let out a sigh of relief. He knew what to do but it seemed so complicated to have to do it all with your feet. It was like trying to write with your toes instead of your fingers. He looked in his mirror to check on the driver and saw him dive into a phone box.

This was not good. Once he called his friends they'd whistle up some help from the police. Alex had to take evasive action. If he went with the traffic he'd still be vulnerable.

He leaned on the horn and revved the engine. The van gathered speed. He passed a taxi and a car. He beeped again. Maybe that was the trick: just go fast and expect everyone else to get out of your way. He was doing fifty-five k.p.h., but the engine sounded a bit hysterical in the low gear.

Ahead, in the bleary gloom, was a set of traffic lights. Alex prayed they would stay green. A bike nipped in front of him and he had to stand on the brakes. He could feel the wheels slipping in the wet and the van stalled again. Alex cursed and restarted it. The lights were red, but a filter to the right was showing green. Very well, that's where he'd go. It was better to keep moving. With one hand on the horn, he hopped across the lane and turned off.

He didn't know where he'd make for, or even where he was. Once he'd got well away from where he'd abandoned the driver, he'd stop and call Hex to arrange an RVP.

The main thing now was that he had Bina and was taking her to safety.

Paulo didn't know how much longer he could hold on. Despite the tourniquet, some of the drug was getting through. He wasn't as co-ordinated as he should be; he rummaged through the stores in the fridge with his free hand and it felt like it belonged to someone else. He swept boxes clumsily to the floor. They were labelled with drug names he'd never heard of.

Then one name he recognized: adrenaline. Hospitals used it when people had severe allergic reactions or cardiac arrests. It might counter the effects of a sedative. It was dangerous – Paulo had enough first-aid training to know that. But if they both blacked out now, after what they had seen, they might never come to.

He tore the end off the box with his teeth and shook out its contents. A pre-loaded syringe clattered to the floor. Should he give it to Amber or take it himself?

He looked at Amber. She stared back groggily. She must be a couple of stone lighter than him – so the drug would have more effect if he gave it to her.

Paulo tried to straighten up but fell over instead. The drug was definitely creeping through his system. His left arm had gone to sleep. It was like a dead weight, floppy and heavy, as if made of rubber. He would have to loosen the tourniquet soon. But when he looked at Amber he realized how powerful the sedative must be; if he hadn't made the tourniquet he would be like her – unable to move.

'Amber, listen,' he said. 'Can you hear me?'

She nodded.

He put the syringe between his teeth, grasped the trolley with his good arm and hauled himself up to sit next to her. He took the syringe in his hand, took the cover off with his teeth and spat it away. 'Amber, listen. I'm going to collapse in a minute. I'll give you this adrenaline and you'll have just a short time to make an escape.'

He looked at the syringe. Where should he inject it? On the tube were the letters IM. Intramuscular. Good; any big muscle would do. He jabbed the injector downwards into the muscular part of Amber's thigh. His left arm was an awkward, rubbery weight underneath him. He could put his whole weight on it and not feel a thing. He couldn't wait any longer. He reached over with his right arm and loosened the tourniquet.

Amber managed to speak. Her lips moved, but no other part of her body did. 'What am I supposed to do, the van's moving.'

Paulo saw her torpor with dismay. Had he given her enough? Should he give her another shot? He felt pins and needles starting in his arm. It was agony, but worse was knowing the drug would claim him in moments. But then he saw her twitch, as though an electric current had passed through her. Was it working?

Amber was suddenly on her feet. Her head thrummed. Her heart raced. One moment she had been fit for nothing, limp as a rag doll. Now it was as though she had been started with jump leads. She felt like running, fast. Paulo slumped down on the trolley, his brown eyes looking up at her.

'Paulo,' said Amber, 'what shall I do?'

When Paulo replied, it was like he was speaking in slow motion. 'Just do something.' His voice was quiet, almost a whisper. 'Just get out, get help.'

Amber looked around wildly. 'What about you?'

Paulo's face was squashed by the hard vinyl cushion of the trolley, It made his lips a strange shape and the words came out as though his mouth was full. 'No . . . time. Find me later.' Then he closed his eyes.

Amber looked at the doors. *Get out*, said her brain. *Get out get out get out.* She tried to think. Where *were* they?

It was raining – she could hear it. How fast was the van going? Hard to tell; the rain was so heavy it drowned any other noise. How long would the adrenaline last? She might conk out again at any minute.

The van braked suddenly, throwing Amber to the floor. The adrenaline in her system said this was it. She sprang up and threw her shoulder to the door. It swung open and she felt rain on her face like a hot shower.

A pair of arms caught her.

Amber tried to run but more arms grabbed her. It took a lot of them, but they pinned her down. She twisted ferociously and caught a glimpse of something that made her blood run cold: the khaki shirt of a police uniform.

* * *

Alex drove on. Progress was slow, even with one hand permanently on the horn. He was still too close to where he had left the driver; he had to get further away. An articulated lorry passed him, sending up a large bow wave of water like a ship. The wheels of the van lost traction and Alex surfed helplessly towards the wrong side of the road. A taxi floated towards him on a direct collision course, its driver beeping while his other hand wrenched the steering wheel. At the last moment Alex slipped past him and the tyres bumped onto the kerb. At last they had something to bite on. Alex floored the accelerator and the van stalled. Alex cursed and started the engine again.

There was a narrow side street to the left. If he could get down there he might make up some distance. He wheeled the van round. The back end skidded out. In his wing mirror he saw he had created a giant wave that sent a bicycle rickshaw floating into a market stall. 'Sorry,' muttered Alex.

But at least he was alone on the road. He accelerated hard, even managing third gear. At the end he could see more traffic on another busy road. He looked in his mirrors: no one was following. There was just a choppy wake like two ploughed furrows. Good. If he could find a few more roads like this he'd make some progress. He changed down a gear roughly and the engine made a howling protest. 'Oh shut up,' he said.

Then, ahead, Alex saw what he didn't want to see. A police car turned into the end of the road and came towards him. Its headlights were flashing alternately and the wail of the siren rose like a cry above the roar of the rain.

He'd have to go back. There was no way out of the alley and no way to turn round. He braked and the wheels skidded on the wet road. The van stalled and carried on for a good hundred metres before stopping. He started the engine again and rammed it into reverse. He looked into his rear-view mirror and saw another police car coming up behind. He was trapped.

Alex yanked on the handbrake and climbed into the back of the van. He had to get Bina out. If Chopra got her again they'd be back to square one. 'Bina, we've got to go.'

Bina stirred slowly. She had been asleep. Alex pulled her up into a sitting position and shook her. Her eyes opened blearily. Even though she had been talking to him fairly normally earlier, the drug must still be in her system. What could he do?

He could get away on his own – he was a fast runner and must be a lot more nimble than the policemen. But with a drugged girl as well?

There was a scrabbling at the door. This is it, thought Alex. The door opened and two policemen were pointing guns into the interior of the van. Could he fight off two at once? With guns? How many more were there?

Alex heard more police getting into the front. They'd definitely taken control of the vehicle. Any minute now Sergeant Chopra would turn up and his fate would be sealed.

One of the policemen climbed in, looked closely at Alex and lowered his gun. 'Are you all right?'

This wasn't what Alex was expecting. Was it a trick? His blood was hammering in his temples. He was ready to fight, to run, but he wasn't ready for this.

The policeman repeated his question. 'Sahib, are you all right? We heard reports that you were in danger.'

Alex nodded. 'Yes. I'm all right.' What was going on?

The policeman in the front turned off the engine. 'All clear in here, sir.' He splashed out into the street.

Alex said, 'Where's Sergeant Chopra?'

The policeman put his gun back into the maroon leather holster. 'Sergeant Chopra is under arrest on charges of corruption. Thanks to your friends.'

Slowly Alex allowed himself to believe it. It was all over. These were good, honest policemen. He and Bina were in safe hands. They'd done it.

He let out a great sigh and sat down on the trolley. Bina stirred a little but carried on sleeping. 'What about Amber and Paulo?' he asked suddenly. 'They were taken prisoner.'

The policeman grinned. 'We sent another unit to find them. The girl Amber is quite a fighter. She broke an officer's nose. It took four men to hold her down. They're at the police station now being examined. The driver is in custody for kidnap. What happened to the driver of this vehicle?'

'I threw him out,' said Alex. 'Back at a junction somewhere.'

'Ah, that explains a phone call we got on Sergeant Chopra's mobile. So who was driving it after that?'

Alex hung his head sheepishly. 'I was.'

'Well, sahib,' said the policeman, 'your driving is diabolical.'

33
CORNERED

When the policeman found him under the tarpaulin, Hex had given himself up immediately. You couldn't argue with a man who had a gun. So he stood up and put his hands in the air. In one hand was his mobile.

'Now you're thinking straight,' the policeman had said. 'Whatever you've done, it's not worth getting shot for.'

Sergeant Chopra came over. Hex looked at the fat, lumbering figure with hatred. Three officers stood around him: the one with the gun and two others.

'This man is a crook,' said Hex acidly.

'Enough of your mischief,' said Sergeant Chopra, laughing off Hex's remark. 'I think we'll get you safely under lock and key. This building site is private property and you're trespassing. You'd better tell your little bouncing friend to join us. Unless you'd like us to shoot her for resisting arrest.'

Hex waved the hand that held his mobile. 'I'll call her.'

Sergeant Chopra nodded and smiled pleasantly. When he was in control of a situation he liked to appear a paragon of reason and politeness.

Hex hit a key on his phone and turned it round so the officer with the gun could see the screen. It showed Sergeant Chopra on the phone to Trilok. The policeman's voice boomed out of the speaker: 'Trilok, you kidnapped that girl and I'm trying to clean up after you. Sometimes it gets messy. That's what you pay me for. And by the way, I'm thinking of putting up my prices.'

Sergeant Chopra had gone a curious grey colour. He made a grab for Hex's phone, but the policeman with the gun cut him off. The sergeant found himself looking into the barrel.

'With respect, Sergeant,' said the officer, 'is that you?'

For a moment it looked as though Chopra would deny everything. Then he heard a click. Another policeman behind him had got out his weapon and taken off the safety catch. He was surrounded.

He nodded slowly.

Hex felt a glow of satisfaction as Chopra finally had to own up to what he'd been up to. But he couldn't relax until he knew the others were out of danger. 'Am I still under arrest?' he said.

The officer shook his head vehemently. 'No, sahib, of course not.'

Hex brought out his palmtop. 'In that case, I need to find out what the sergeant has done with my friends.'

With the help of Hex's tracking devices, it had been easy to pinpoint where the others were, and officers were sent to rescue them.

Alpha Force were reunited at Chennai police

headquarters, a modern building with air conditioning – very different from the tatty local station presided over by Sergeant Chopra. They had been examined by the police doctor and now sat giving statements around a big table in a plush office. Li and Hex had stopped off at the hostel on the way to collect the suitcase of documents. Now they spread them out on the table, file after file of evidence.

'This is terrific,' said the investigating officer. 'Everything's here – all the people Trilok's been bribing, all the people he's been cheating. How did you get hold of all this?'

'We found it lying around,' said Hex quickly. He couldn't very well tell the police they'd picked the lock of Trilok's flat and gone snooping. This was often the difficult bit of an operation: covering up the dubious means by which they had brought the villains to justice.

The investigating officer gave Hex a look. Then the police doctor came in – and if the officer had been going to say something, he soon forgot about it.

'Mind if I join you?' said the doctor. 'I've

examined Bina and she's OK – just a bit hung over.'

'Have a look at these files,' said the investigating officer. 'See what you make of them.'

Alex was looking at Amber and Paulo with concern. They were slumped back in their chairs, watching the proceedings with bleary eyes. Amber had been wide awake when they were examined by the doctor but now she looked deflated.

Alex touched the doctor on the arm. 'Er, Doctor, have you seen . . .'

The doctor looked at Amber and Paulo, then said: 'They're fine. They were given diazepam and it often stays in your system. You think you've recovered and then you get another drowsy period. That's probably why they used it on Bina; so that if she came round a bit early or they didn't give her the next dose in time, she'd go off again all by herself. It'll wear off.' She looked at Paulo. 'By the way, you were lucky you didn't kill Amber with that adrenaline. Give the wrong dose and you could have stopped her heart.'

'*Dios*,' said Paulo. 'I don't think I'll do that again.'

Li took the strange pair of scissors she had found in the morgue out of her backpack and handed them to the doctor. 'We found these on our travels. What are they?'

The doctor picked them up and turned them over. 'Enucleation scissors.' He was met by blank looks so he translated: 'For taking out eyes.' He put them down again.

Amber, although half asleep, still registered what the doctor had said. 'Ewww. Put them away.'

Hex picked them up and flew them past Amber as if they were a toy plane. He snipped the jaws experimentally.

She swatted his hand. 'Pack it in. I may be nearly asleep but nightmares make me violent.'

Hex grinned and put the scissors down again.

The doctor was looking at them. 'That's quite a specialist piece of equipment. Doctors don't usually carry them. Where did you find them?'

Li couldn't say she'd picked them up in the local police morgue. 'They were dropped in the street,' she said. 'By that man with the cool box.'

The investigating officer pulled over another file.

'We checked Sergeant Chopra's phone. He was making regular calls to Vikram Medical Supplies. It coincided with whenever an unidentified body was brought into the morgue. He was selling the eyes.'

Alex, Hex and Li exchanged a meaningful look.

Hex indicated Trilok's files: 'We can't find anything about that in here, though.'

'No.' The investigating officer shook his head. 'It's not connected with Trilok. But Sergeant Chopra's confessed. He was selling to the eye bank and receiving payments from Trilok to protect him. When you turned up looking for Bina, he called his friends at Vikram and had her put in one of their vans. So he'll be arrested for corruption and abetting an abduction.'

Paulo yawned. 'Where is Trilok?'

Li grinned. 'The police tracked him using his mobile. He was in Mount Road but when we looked out in the street we couldn't see him. So I called his number and waited to see where the sound came from.'

Hex was grinning too. 'He was right outside the

General Medical Ethics Committee building. In a dustbin.'

They all laughed. Even Paulo and Amber chuckled quietly. 'Very appropriate,' drawled Amber in what was almost a whisper.

Hex found it strange to have her operating at half volume. He patted her head. 'I rather like this new, quiet Amber. She's like a pussycat.'

'Watch out,' said Amber sotto voce. 'I may be cute but I bite.'

The investigating officer told them, 'We've got Trilok downstairs in the cells and those files will be very useful.' He looked at the doctor. 'What do you make of them, Doctor?'

The police doctor looked up. 'The test results are rather interesting. There are a lot in one kind of handwriting that are complete nonsense. They can't have been done by anyone with medical knowledge.'

Li replied, 'We think he was looking for people who had been refused transplants. He'd tell them he would find them a kidney and get them to keep paying for tests until they died.'

The doctor's face was grave. 'Yes, that could well

be what was going on here. How despicable.' The contempt in his voice was clear.

'What I don't understand is why he kept them,' said Hex. 'All those reports in his own handwriting are incriminating.'

'I think I can help with that,' said the doctor. 'He's faking the names of the donors, so he has to make sure he doesn't duplicate them. Otherwise the patient might spot that they've already paid for a match test with, for example, a Mrs Patel of Egmore Road.'

Alex looked at the investigating officer. 'What will happen to Trilok and Chopra? Will they go to jail?'

The officer shrugged. 'Chopra definitely. He's confessed. The committee members will probably be struck off and fined. But Trilok . . . he's saying nothing, he's demanded to talk to his lawyer. With all this evidence, we can make a good case. But he's a rich man and he has rich friends.'

Alex smiled wryly. 'And he obviously knows about bribing government officials.'

The investigating officer nodded. 'We'll do what we can.'

The doctor was riffling through papers. 'Interesting,' he said loudly. 'Look at these.' He spread the papers out so everyone could see.

The pages were from a private hospital. In the space that said 'Patient's name' was written 'Tagore Trilok'.

Having looked through so many similar papers, Hex had an idea of what they might be. He looked at the doctor. 'Are these tests done on Trilok?'

The doctor nodded. 'These are kidney function tests. Genuine ones – I know the consultant who's signed them. It looks like Trilok's suffering from kidney disease.'

Li turned to Paulo. 'You found that drug wrapper,' she said. 'And you said he didn't look well.'

The doctor nodded. 'Looking at these it's not surprising. Within a year, he's going to be very ill indeed. Whether he's in jail or not he's going to need all that money he made.'

34
END OF A
LONG DAY

Alex, Li and Hex opened the door to their room in the hostel. A few hours earlier they had brought Bina, Amber and Paulo back so that they could sleep off the effects of the drugs properly.

Alex peeked in. The room was dark. He turned back to the others. 'They're still asleep,' he hissed.

As if to confirm this, a loud snore came from the room.

'That's got to be Paulo,' said Li.

'I bet it's Amber,' said Hex.

'Lazy louts,' said Alex. 'They've had a couple of hours.' He, Li and Alex had spent the time at the police station, helping the officers sort through all the evidence and providing other evidence of their own.

'So what shall we do, put the light on?'

Suddenly the lights came on on their own. There was a great chorus of 'Surprise!'

Alex, Li and Hex whirled round. Standing behind the door – and very much awake – were Bina, Amber and Paulo.

But they weren't alone. Bina's whole family were there – Mootama, Naresh, and her sisters Radha and Sami.

Naresh stepped forward and shook Alex solemnly by the hand. He didn't say anything, just gave his hand a firm shake and held it for a moment. Then he moved on to Hex, shaking his hand and holding it before releasing it.

Li expected she would be next and went forwards to offer her hand, but Amber gave her a look that said *No*. Li remembered. There were strict rules about when Indian men could touch women, and that included shaking hands.

Naresh let Hex go and stood in front of Li. He didn't need to shake her hand; his eyes said it all.

Alex recovered from the surprise first. 'How did you get here?'

Amber answered. 'I wasn't tired, so I made some phone calls. Paulo had the number of the phone in Nayla and they got a message to Mootama.'

Mootama took up the story. 'Pradesh was coming into town to pick up materials. He offered to bring us in and pick us up later.'

Amber sniffed. 'What's that smell?'

Alex and Li fetched a couple of large baskets from outside the door. 'We brought a takeaway. The police recommended a restaurant.'

'Not the one Sergeant Chopra goes to,' added Li quickly with a shudder. Her four friends laughed.

Amber's eyes lit up. 'Fab.' She clambered across the bed and opened one of the baskets. Inside were smaller baskets, their contents wrapped in napkins. She unfolded one and saw little chunks of marinaded lamb. It smelled delicious. Another contained a porcelain bowl with a fragrant dish of lentils and spices.

Li hefted another two baskets in from outside the door. 'There's plenty here,' she said to Mootama and the others. 'Do please join us.'

Naresh looked at his eldest daughter. 'I don't think we'll be able to leave for a while anyway.'

Bina looked as though she would swoon with bliss. 'I haven't eaten proper food for days.' Now she had got rid of the surgical gown and the police had found her a clean sari, she looked like a normal, healthy teenager again.

They laid a bedspread on the floor and put the food out on it, like a picnic, then they all sat down to eat. Naresh and Mootama ate only sparingly, preferring to watch as Bina attacked the feast. Sami and Radha insisted on sitting on either side of Paulo and acting as his own personal waitresses, passing him dishes faster than he could eat. They were so intent on feeding him that they hardly bothered to eat anything themselves.

What is this effect he has on girls? wondered Li.

For a while the only sounds in the room were the sounds of enjoyment. Alpha Force tucked in, eating the south Indian way – making a small handful of rice into a ball and dipping it into a sauce.

Amber poked Hex in the ribs. 'By the way, I do not snore.'

'You do,' said Hex. He looked round to see Radha watching them intently. 'She was snoring in the police station,' he explained to her. 'Like a buzz saw.'

'Rubbish,' said Amber. Her phone rang and she glanced at the screen. 'I'll deal with you later,' she said to Hex severely, then moved away from the party to take the call.

Radha looked at Hex intently. 'Are you and Amber married?'

Hex's eyes nearly popped out of his head. Then he realized he wasn't the only person who'd been dumbstruck. Everyone else had gone quiet too.

Bina was toying with a chapatti, her appetite gone. Mootama and Naresh gave each other uncomfortable looks. Paulo, Li and Alex looked down into their plates, not knowing what to say.

Of course, thought Hex. It's like we thought all along. We may have rescued Bina, but nobody knows what to do about her dowry – or dowries for the other girls. Radha's cheeky remark had brought into the open the problem that nobody wanted to think about. But hopefully the school would change all that, wouldn't it?

Hex asked: 'How's Pradesh getting on fitting out the school?'

'It's now got electricity,' said Naresh. 'Soon we will be ready for furniture and equipment. But we'll get our teacher through the aid programme and they've told us it will take at least twelve months.'

Alex caught the tone in Naresh's voice. It was the tone of a man who had been beating his head against a brick wall – Alex had felt just the same when he had tried to get a doctor for the young boy. Bina was now thirteen. Many of the girls were married at twelve. The family wouldn't be able to wait another year to see what happened with the school, they would have to get her married off soon or she would be too old. And Radha would be coming up to marriageable age soon.

Suddenly, Alex felt very tired. Everything they had gone through, everything he had been inspired to do since seeing that TV report, turned to dust. He had hoped they would change lives, but all they'd leave behind was an empty building.

Amber finished her call and rejoined the party. She was shocked to see the circle of sombre faces.

Mootama reached over and patted Bina's hand in an attempt to reassure her. Amber understood that gesture: it was trying to say everything would be all right, even if she had no idea how.

Amber sat down next to Hex again. 'I've just been talking to my uncle John in the States,' she said. 'He's got a friend with a multinational company who was thinking of setting up a big call centre. You know, when you phone up to buy more mobile phone time and you think you're talking to someone just downtown? Well, usually they're actually somewhere like the Far East or Pakistan. Anyway, Uncle John's just persuaded him to locate it in Chennai. It'll take them a year to kit it out, but it means that kids just coming out of school can walk straight into jobs.'

Everyone nodded, looking impressed. But their response was lukewarm, as though they were just trying to be polite. Not as if she'd just dropped an amazing bombshell.

'What's up?' said Amber. 'Did I leave out the bit

about them employing nearly four hundred people?'

It was Alex who answered. 'The problem is, the aid programme can't send a teacher for twelve months.' The others nodded.

'Oh, I sorted that as well,' said Amber. 'Uncle said they'd need specific training anyway. The company will get grants because they're preparing pupils to work in emerging technologies. They can sponsor a teacher and send him or her over as soon as you like.'

At last the news seemed to go down well. Amber could feel the tension in the room melt away. Mootama and Naresh looked at each other, tears in their eyes.

Paulo and Hex resumed joking with the two younger girls; Alex and Li were challenging each other to eat the two fieriest dishes on the table. Amber felt very happy. Her uncle had powerful friends and although she didn't like to rely on them, she had to admit there were times when they were very, very useful.

Paulo looked at Radha and Sami. 'So in a few years' time, when I'm trying to top up calltime, I might be speaking to one of you guys.'

'Or me,' said Bina, grinning broadly. Her appetite had returned and she dug a chapatti into the vegetable curry.

'No, me,' said Sami. She saw Bina mopping up more food and swiped the bowl of lentils, offering it to Paulo.

'No, no more,' said Paulo helplessly. 'I'm full to here.' He put his hand over the top of his head.

'Give it to me,' said Bina.

'No,' said Radha, 'you've had loads. Give it to' – she looked around to see who she wanted to bestow her favours on next – 'give it to Alex.'

Alex saw the lentils advancing towards him and shook his head, his eyes bulging and watering. His hands fanned his mouth as though he'd eaten a hot coal. He grabbed a bottle of water and downed the whole lot.

It was another few moments before he could speak. 'Phew, that was hot. I think I am going to need a transplant.'

'Why?' said Li.

Alex wiped his eyes. 'Dodgy tikka.'

CHRIS RYAN'S TOP SAS TACTICS ON STREET SURVEILLANCE

In *Blood Money*, Alpha Force use all their street surveillance skills to follow the crooked agent around Chennai. And in a country where they can easily stand out simply because of their ethnic origin, they really do need skills. As a member of the SAS, I have often had to follow someone as part of the intelligence-gathering stage of a mission, and there are some basic rules that are worth keeping in mind if you ever need to follow someone yourself.

Do remember, however, that these skills are *for*

serious operations only, where it is necessary to gain vital intelligence. *Never follow anyone unnecessarily*. It can be very scary to discover someone is following you – and if you are spotted following a stranger, you could be putting yourself into danger. So these skills should only be practised with your mates. This will mean that your skills will really have to honed well as your friend is very likely to spot you!

Here are my top ten SAS tactics for following someone in an urban environment:

1. Teamwork

To avoid being spotted it is best to operate as a team. Obviously, the more people you have, the more you can vary who's following. One of you follows for ten minutes, then the other takes over. When I worked on a surveillance operation in Scotland following a guy for over a week, we had a team of three, on foot and in cars. If our target stopped, the person following would keep on walking and overtake them. Someone else then took up the pursuit.

If you're in a team, communications are vital. We kept in touch by radio and earpiece, but you could use mobile phones. One of your team is the controller: he or she knows where everybody is and can plot where the target might go next. When we were in Scotland, we marked up local maps with zones – red, yellow, green and so on. When we needed to tell the controller where the target was going, we'd say, 'In yellow five moving to green three' – and if anyone was listening they'd have no idea what we were doing. If the target disappears, the controller can look at the map and send people to block off where he might be.

You might want to use hand signals, in which case make sure you all know exactly what they mean. Each team member could be represented by a different finger on your hand – so if you put one finger up to scratch your ear, you mean for Team Member A to take over; three fingers could mean Team Member C; and so on. If you work as part of a team – like Alpha Force – you will soon develop a range of ways of communicating with each other without needing specific equipment.

Let everyone share the workload. The longer that just one person follows the target, the more likely they are to be spotted. Don't try to be a hero and follow them yourself all day – swap regularly.

2. Know your area

Try to get to know the area you will be working in before the operation starts. It certainly won't help if you get lost as you won't be able to report the target's position back to team-mates! Look for places that may cause problems. For example, a street market may be filled with people and it is worth knowing if your target is heading in that direction as you will need to move closer to avoid losing them. If you *do* lose them, knowing the surroundings means you can scoot on ahead, say to the other shopping mall exit, and be ready to pick them up when they reappear.

There may be times when you'll need to look at your map, but don't do it in full view of everybody – duck into a shop.

3. Useful items

Again, if you have advance warning, there are

practical items you can take with you that may make the difference between success and failure. For example, take some loose change in case you have to follow a suspect onto a bus. You'd feel pretty silly if you lost your target simply because you had failed to make sure you had the bus fare!

A mobile phone is always useful, but a phone card or change may be vital if you are in an area where the signal is poor.

And make sure you are wearing comfortable and appropriate clothes and shoes or boots. If the furthest you normally walk is to the bus stop and back, a three-hour walk following someone could give you blisters! And you'd be pretty uncomfortable, too, if you set off in a T-shirt and it poured with rain.

4. Blend into your surroundings

There's a saying: *When in Rome, do as the Romans do*, and this certainly applies to surveillance. When I was in Scotland, we looked at what the locals were wearing and tried to blend in. That's another reason to visit the area beforehand – you'd really stand out if you wore sports gear and they were all in business suits. Alpha Force are at a disadvantage in Chennai because they don't look like the local race. Their untouchable costume does two jobs – allows them to blend in while covering their distinctive hair and skin colour.

Many people think that you should always wear a disguise. This all depends on how well the subject you are following knows you – and how good you are at disguising yourself. A large false nose or a silly hat will only make you stand out in a crowd. Instead, disguise yourself with 'normal' things – a baseball cap, a coat that is different from the kind you normally wear, glasses or sunglasses will all make a big difference. You don't have to use them all at once: first try a pair of glasses, then swap these for a baseball cap, and finally try a different coloured top. But how you move is probably even more important; as Paulo knows, many people have a distinctive way of walking or using their hands or other gestures that make them recognizable. Try copying the way your mates walk and you will realize how much of this kind of thing you do notice yourself. Then ask them to copy you and you will know what you will need to disguise!

Try not to do anything to draw attention to yourself. If everyone is sauntering along a road, for instance, a quick sprint would be an excellent way of making sure everyone looks at you. If you decide it's time for a different look, don't put on your glasses in the street; pop into a shop and change. And you might try to disguise your normal way of walking or standing, but a Quasimodo imitation may draw admirers who think you are part of a street theatre, rather than let you get on with the job in hand.

Never make eye contact with your target. If you make eye contact with someone, they notice you – and usually wonder why you're staring at them! They'll certainly remember you after that and your cover will be blown.

Oh, and make sure you are aware of your surroundings, too, and not just focused on a target. Walking slap into a lamppost isn't just a great way of being noticed by everyone around you; it also hurts!

5. Know your target's routine

A bit of research might save you a lot of legwork. In Scotland we went through our target's bins and learned a lot about him. Till receipts, cheque stubs, credit card bills and letters told us all the places he liked to go to. I followed him around Sainsbury's one day. While he was shopping, his mobile rang, so I moved a bit closer to listen to what he was saying.

6. Keep the right distance

Don't get too close to your subject – nor so far away that you lose them. Remember how easy it is in a city to turn a corner and discover a crowd, though, so be flexible. How close you go will depend on how many other people are around, what time of day or night it is, whether you are working alone or as part of a team, and all sorts of other factors. Girls can often get a bit closer to the target than guys because they don't seem so threatening.

Vary your position behind a suspect. If, for instance, you begin by following along from the opposite side of the street, try crossing over at some point so that you are on the same side – a target will be less likely to notice you if you are not always in the same position. If they stop sometimes, overtake and then pause to look in a shop window before continuing behind once they have passed you again.

7. Act naturally

Use the local surroundings to act as natural as possible. If you're in a shopping area, look in the windows. Buy a newspaper outside a station. Do all the ordinary things that others are doing, and this will also help to vary your pace and make you less noticeable.

You might find it helpful to have a prop or two. A female team-member might carry a handbag (a make-up mirror is excellent for seeing behind you, too) or you could have a sports bag to rummage in. Do make sure that anything you are carrying is inconspicuous and won't make you stand out. Tip: carry an *empty* sports bag to rummage in and dump it during the operation. It is amazing how many people would notice you as 'person with bag' and then see someone totally different if suddenly you are without the bag.

If you act naturally it's surprising what you can get away with. Again, on the mission in Scotland, the target had meetings in a café every morning. The café was always full. I walked in, bought a coffee and looked for somewhere to sit. There were two extra chairs at the table where the target was sitting, so I walked up and asked, 'Mind if I sit here?' I was told, 'Go ahead.' So I sat down, got out my magazine and pretended to read. Actually I was listening to everything that was said – what the target was up to and where he was going. This meant we didn't even have to follow the target for the rest of the day! I had to be careful only to show my left side, though – in my right ear I had an earpiece I was using to communicate with the others and if the target had seen that the whole mission might have been blown. You have to be constantly aware of who's around you and what they can see.

8. Be very careful how you start

You're most likely to be rumbled when you're starting a surveillance operation. If you sit outside the target's house waiting for them to come out, a neighbour might spot you and call the police before you've gone anywhere. If you wait at their usual bus stop, but never get on a bus, it also looks suspicious. It might be better to start covertly – hide in a bush outside the target's house and radio to your mates when they come out.

9. When it goes wrong . . .

If you think the target has spotted you, act as naturally as possible and do everything possible to make them doubt their suspicion.

Walk past, catch a bus without looking back – anything to make them feel they were wrong to feel they were being followed.

Tell the others in your team so that someone else can take over. If you are working alone, accept that you have lost the target and be prepared to try again another day.

Always pull off if you're not sure – otherwise

you might ruin the whole mission.

Be very aware of what *you* would do if you spotted someone following you. Would you test them by doubling back on yourself? Cross the road, and then cross back again? If your target begins doing any of these things, they may simply be being careful – but it is far more likely they have spotted you. Try to hand over to a team member in a non-suspicious manner and then abandon the pursuit yourself.

Your target might even try actively to lose you. The classic way of doing this is to go into a department store – they can lose you in the crowds and there are often too many exits for you to cover.

10. Avoid danger

Most important of all, under no circumstances do anything that could put you in danger of any kind. If the target seems to be leading you into shadowy areas or dead-ends, don't take the bait. Better to withdraw and wait for support from team members than to take any kind of risk. This is vital. Most